SEATTLE

or

IN THE MEANTIME

SEATTLE

or

IN THE MEANTIME

a novel

J.M. PARKER

Beautiful Dreamer Press

Seattle, or In the Meantime
Copyright 2020 by Joshua M. Parker

Beautiful Dreamer Press
309 Cross Street
Nevada City, CA 95959
U.S.A.
www.BeautifulDreamerPress.com
info@BeautifulDreamerPress.com

This is a work of fiction. All characters, places, and incidents are the products of the author's imagination. Although some names, places, and events are referred to for historical context, all are used fictitiously. Any resemblance to actual events, locales, or persons, living or dead, is entirely coincidental.

Adapted excerpts of this novel have appeared in *Callisto* and *Interdisciplinary Studies in Literature and Environment.*

Paperback Edition
10 9 8 7 6 5 4 3 2
Publication date: March 2021
Printed in the United States of America

ISBN: 978-1-7347389-3-3
Library of Congress Control Number: 2020944085

Cover design by Tom Schmidt
Cover photo by Julia Mullikin

To O.

Contents

SEATTLE

or

IN THE MEANTIME

. . . not knowing how to swim or skate, he could say: *I skate and I swim*—and, magically, everyone had seen him on the ice and in the water. He took no precautions, had no calculations to make. His face was never perturbed. A special fairy casts this spell at birth. Some, to whose cradle no other fairy comes but this, succeed.

—Jean Cocteau, *Thomas the Impostor*

1991, the last year of the 20th century

—Alexis Jenni, *L'Art français de la guerre*

Forward

Light on the Pacific Northwest coast is a translucent white, mornings. Fog filters out yellows like a photographer's screen then, rising, leaves a landscape sharp and gray as an Ansel Adams. Our first views of the Hudson Valley, the Great Plains and California we owe to painters and sketchers, but our first images of the Washington and British Columbian coast are clean Daguerreotypes etched on steel plates not much more than a hundred years ago. Or those fabulous creatures painted by Coast Salish peoples since the time when animals became men, stark as wood prints, flashing blocks of neon outlined in black.

Once, I lived on the back of a hill so steep that the freeway just below our building was invisible from the windows. Leaning from the dining room, craning your head just right into the traffic's low buzz, you saw a slim gray slab of Puget Sound above the shrubbery. The stretch between our hill and the Sound was once the base of another hill. A hundred years earlier, when the city found it too cumbersome to pull cable cars up and down its side, it was bulldozed and hydro-powered away. For seventy years the resulting flatland sprawled out, proliferating carwashes and laundromats, till it was cut off from our hill by the freeway. Left to waste like a half-amputated limb, its northern edge sank toward Lake Union, breezes from the lake filtering through four lanes of traffic and a shallow field where wild geese gathered year-round to molt and shit on the grass. Condominiums rose to the west. Squinting at them offered the illusion of a low valley between Belltown and Capitol Hill, even though it must be the flattest part of town. The *Fishing and Hunting News* editorial offices had dusty windowsills and perpetually drawn blinds. A small, evidently nameless cafe, open late, had cheap, good espresso, a tattered couch and a view of the expressway off-ramp and the lake's clustered houseboats, where errant lawyers gathered at dusk to drink wine and plan sailing trips. From their docks you could see our building, down the hill from the cathedral, perched in discreet brick walks, forests of ferns and mansions. Directly below us, the building dropped fifty feet to a private, secluded wasteland of shattered cinderblock and brambles, discarded relics of summer yard sales poking out through ivy, cedar stumps, and great cords of thrashed broken thorny branches tossed from the terrace of our landlady's rose garden.

I stood in the brambles' afternoon shade, picking blackberries, listening to the rush of cars, the cawing of crows in the cedars above the waste, the occasional angry splutter of a motorcycle climbing toward Broadway, where kids from Bellevue tattooed themselves and read Hare Krishna tracts, or got someone to buy them beer, hanging out behind the Taco Bell, daring each other to light joints between the parking lot's Audis. The true homeless people stayed off Broadway. They spent their days wandering, silently unpacking the contents of garbage dumpsters in empty alleys, when they could find dumpsters that weren't locked.

One of them, a man, used to make his way up our hill from the freeway just at dusk, regular as clockwork. I sat on a bench by the landlady's roses, watching the Space Needle's beacon flash Jetsonesque promises from its seismographically-sound spire. I liked to wait till the last dip of sunlight passed through the valley of ruined garages at the Needle's base, its glowing, empty streets lighting with neon and halogen. He had the same habit, settling on the bench beside mine. There was dirt in the wrinkles around his eyes. He smoked a pipe that stank of scorched tobacco and something else—dirt, or dry leaves, or hair. Sometimes he'd ask for a cigarette, mashing it into his pipe, and we'd sit together smoking by the landlady's roses, admiring the view, while he made the kind of remarks someone with untreated schizophrenia might be expected to make. Sometimes he talked about Vietnam, a word I'd always imagined as an historical period, but which for him was a place where you sweated at night watching things burn. Sometimes he talked about angels and devils, sometimes about Indian temples submerged under Elliott Bay. Once, he explained how he got to Seattle—hitchhiking or on buses or trains—after realizing where he was from when he saw the Space Needle in a Manhattan bookstore window, setting off toward the Holland Tunnel entrance to find his way home, guided by voices. One night, as we sat looking over the city, he asked what I did for a living.

"Not much," I'd said.

"You must do something to live in a place like that," he pressed, pointing his pipe at the steel door of the building's service entrance, set deep in the brick, framed with its lattice of roses, into which by now he knew I disappeared once the sun was down.

"Not really," I said.

But my vagueness had roused his lucidity. "Everybody is something. What do you do for work?" I figured if a homeless schizophrenic could muster enough coherence to interest himself in someone else's domestic situation, he deserved an honest answer.

"I fuck a lawyer." It was the first honest thing I'd said to anyone in a while. It left a spooky feeling inside me.

"Hmph," he muttered, motionless, staring out at our view.

Behind us, a sports car rounded the cul-de-sac at full

speed, passing our bench with a hollow thump of bass. A wailing shriek followed as it pulled off—the cat from the Chinese grocer's down the block had panicked crossing in its path. In a black pool glistening under the streetlight, its fur was matted on the asphalt. It didn't move as we walked over to it, so we found a stick and dragged the dead cat into the bushes behind the grocery. The sun had sunk. Neither of us wanted to stand in the bushes with the dead cat. Neither of us wanted to go back to the bench and sit with our backs to it. So we stood under the streetlight, over the wet stain on the asphalt.

"That guy didn't even slow down," he said.

"I guess it's kind of a tough neighborhood."

"Didn't even slow down," he muttered. His eyes met mine. "Don't kid yourself, buddy, once you lose your soul, you've lost it."

"Can't you just check it at the door and pick it up again later?"

He chuckled. "Maybe," he said. He mused to himself. His eyes twinkled, fixed on the spot between our feet. "But don't expect to get it back like you gave it to them."

MY EXTREMELY POSTMODERN FAMILY

Until I met Isaac, my mother was a college ballet instructor. My father was a concert pianist. My sister was in reform school for four counts of arson. She cried behind a Plexiglas panel when we visited her once a month, pressing her fingers to the glass stained yellow from nicotine, though she was just fourteen. Until I met Isaac, my brother married a Greek princess when I was seven years old. I'd worn a tiny velveteen tuxedo and been ring-bearer on a white yacht. Until I met Isaac, my grandmother, afraid she'd never be able to get silk again during Vietnam, bought up three fabric stores, locked in the basement, scrolled on racks in a specially-ventilated room. My mother, a professional orchid grower, was a passive-aggressive smasher of Wedgewood and Baccarat. My father, in panic attacks, shouted into his broker's answering machine, or leaned across the piano with drunken hands, lulling us awake with Chopin preludes until two in the morning. Until meeting Isaac, I'd never heard the sound of a vacuum cleaner. The cleaning lady did it while I was at school. Before meeting Isaac, I rode to school in a limousine.

On the stairs, a polished banister ran with sentry-like balustrades, light from a Palladian window hitting its curved ridges around four o'clock. Brass chimes rang from a scarred grandfather clock in the hall. A scent of rain and furniture polish rose from magnolias across a blue lawn. Before meeting Isaac, the following faded in the half-light of the Restoration saloon once it was dark enough to switch on the lamps: Ming tureens in teakwood stands, lone goldfish swimming quiet circles in clear water. Adam furniture, a Tiepolo ceiling, immense cabinets of silver epergne. An iron Gothic winter garden, open to a pool edged with milled lapis. Before meeting Isaac, I lied with an earnest faith that anything said cleverly and often enough was true enough. When details didn't please me—many didn't—I made others up.

When the world you describe and the stories you tell are all fabrication, they're your own, more than anything else in the world is ever yours. I never lied too much, like the kid who, pretending to be sick to get out of school, ends up feeling too sick to enjoy freedom after describing his symptoms. My kind of lying was in the details, and I tended to be faithful to details, and after a while they accumulate. So when I try to describe the house I lived in as a child, I'm tempted to lie out of habit.

Photographs, pretending to trigger memories, work a seductive trick of becoming memory. Still, I trust luridly-colored family photo albums more than myself. Here, my early childhood is just another phase in my parents' life, after the cutting of a tiered cake and waving before a car covered in shaving cream, a series of picnics. Sometimes one appears, badly lit, drinking coffee in a bathrobe, smirking at some decades-long forgotten joke. My début (one unsuccessful oeuvre of hospital photography) appears as relevant as the fact that parrots once landed on my mother's shoulder in Key Largo, or that my father grinned on a mountain peak with a pair of binoculars around his neck.

Photographs show: a kitchen with the wallpaper from above Mike and Carol Brady's headboard (an unsavory correspondence noted when I was ten); a chandelier of flat panes of smoked glass; a ceiling textured like pale goose-fleshed skin; a bookcase with a mark near the bottom where the hard plastic tire of a Big Wheel hit it with a good running start; bulbs in vaguely Gothic wrought-iron wall sconces, never lit; trophies hung without wiring. Our father furnished it all from estate sales and flooded hotels, off IRS seizures of Persian businessmen and refurbishments of state Governors' mansions: twisted, bulbous with crystal, waterlogged, inlaid. Couches of awkward dimensions, gilt that rubbed off on your pants legs. Wide rugs lapped at the walls' baseboards, edges folded double beneath them.

Photos don't help. For what it's worth, here's what I calculate as my first honest-to-goodness unphoto-oped memory.

It was early morning. The front door hung open, over-looking a piney golf course marked for development, left to grow wild during the oil crisis and recession. Mist bed-ded the lawn. Nose pressed to the storm door, you could see birds huddled together on the power lines, quiet be-hind the glass. A man had just left. An odor of Grey Flannel lingered in the hall. A matter-of-fact female voice in the room intoned, "In the meantime..."

A car rumbled past the driveway bushes up the hill, echoing in the fog. Looking through the storm door, I pondered the word "meantime." It resonated in the hallway. It's the first word I remember learning. Time had stopped. Turning it over in my mind, I tried to make sense of it. I knew "mean" meant "bad," and "time" meant waiting. There was something ominous about this intermediary time, it seemed clear from the tone of the voice behind me. Nothing I could do would speed it up again.

Velveteen tuxedos, incarcerated sister, and yachts aside, my first memory is of watching the world through a storm door window, penetrated with frustration at not being able to step outside. And the first word I re-member learning seemed to describe the whole thing perfectly.

My mother, a clothes hound, kept subscriptions to *Psychology Today* and *Vogue*, into whose stacks I delved, ogling images of people in worlds both less and more real than ours. *Vogue* offered reviews of French bed and breakfasts where one "escaped" for "the art of the long weekend." How weekends could extend beyond Sundays or Saturdays, I didn't know.

I wandered the woods at the edge of the suburb. Climbing through the open window of a long-defunct local railroad baron's abandoned palace, I paced its empty tiled pool, admired the wreck of its rocaille wall sconces, dumbwaiters, and Moroccan scenes on rotting leather panels, and absorbed an impression I sensed would be transposable long after the place, the lake, and the woods around it were demolished to make way for a shopping center.

There are whole suburbs of America where the main view of the land as it was before you got there is a snatch of oak trees on a vacant lot, a nest of squirrels. Occasional fox tracks, noticed in snow. Only fit to look at if you cultivate the ability to block out the most obvious things: power lines, the night-haze glow of the closest shopping center. Most people, I guess, live in places where forests have been cut and marshes filled in. I suppose there are people who live on landfills. But there's nothing intrinsically wholesome about suburbs in any place. Ours was a lone street at city's edge, two rows of split-level ranches lined up, dumbly facing each other, as if waiting for something. In the woods to either side, with occasional scars in the blood-red clay, some industrious millionaires, seeking privacy, had excavated basements, leaving scattered cinderblocks before business, ruin or scandal led elsewhere, and lichen and brambles returned.

We'd come to the place when it was nearly the country, but there were droning bull-dozers. A dozen McMansions sprouted in clearings. The piney gorge at the end of the street, punctuated by a drafty sheep barn and dusty service station, soon emptied straight into Kensington Heights's swath of glazed terra-cotta cul-de-sacs and rounded brick bends. Kensington's Heights' shopping center and business park rose five minutes away, off a spanking new highway, replete with 500,000 square feet of executive-appointed office space, and the easily-distracted staff of the Kensington Heights Towne Centre Hotel, in whose lobby a teenager might requisition an armchair to lounge unquestioned for hours, or even, with a studied touch of insouciance, take the elevator to swim in the glass-roofed pool.

Grandmothers on both sides of my family died twice each in car accidents, plane crashes, and on ill-fated cruises. I contracted bouts of mononucleosis, had orthodontic complications, cat-scratch fever, and would gladly have reported floods, hurricanes and tornadoes as long as it kept me away from the high school's linoleum, its fluorescent lights. I forged signatures. I forewent textbooks, lying poolside at the Kensington

Heights Towne Centre Hotel with books from the local university library, snagging coffee from the breakfast buffet, making illicit use of the Kensington Heights tennis courts and golf greens, improving my backhand on the former, cultivating an overstated reputation as a womanizer on the latter, and patronizing Kensington Heights Centre's McDonald's for sustenance, pissing on its restroom floor out of vague political convictions, boredom, or spite. Extracurricular activity dropped my GPA, but I was accepted to a decent college, which was evidently the next step.

Living less in reality than in pictures and novels, success depends on how you piece them together, stretch them into a fabric through whose seams all else shows as little and seldom as possible, shadows on translucent pages you regurgitate, a tapestry of your own design. Of experiences you haven't *had*. Yet *have*. Believing in them yourself, even slightly, changes what belief itself means. Life's landmarks, confused with scenes from movies, made it surprisingly difficult to tease out the strands of my own history. Everything seemed uniquely my own, nothing really mine. It took two whole semesters to sort that out, long afternoons on a standard-issue dormitory bed shoved into the chasm of a dormer window, looking at the sky, dragging on cigarettes.

I still harbored secret hopes I might be a genius. I figured I was gay. My roommate was. He went out twice a week to a disco after sitting on the floor blowing pot smoke into a shampoo bottle stuffed with sheets of fabric softener. I didn't dance well, was too young to go to bars. When we passed on sidewalks on the way to classes, he smiled. His friends stood a little behind him, eyeing me suspiciously. "Is he gay? Or is he straight?" they asked.

"He's bi-fucking-sexual," my roommate would snap from across the quad, loud so I could hear him, nodding back.

Finally something happened. You know the dinner party where couples who don't know each other get stuck together at a table? The host suggests you each tell how you and your partner met. Three out of six of you are lying. One couple flubs their communally-concocted tale. Everyone pretends not to notice. A couple collectively screws up their story on purpose, drawing everyone's attention to the ruse of the game. Whichever of the befuddled stories is most romantic, the story told by that one partner who gets everything akimbo is the one really worth hearing.

Here's how we met. In a dark apartment in which the guy whose apartment it was held court fostering rumors he'd been kicked out of the drama department for refusing to cut his hair for a production of *Oklahoma*, I saw this boy Isaac from the religious studies department by the bookcase. A broken desk lamp over a painting of Jesus illuminated his face. Isaac asked for a cigarette. I handed him one. He broke it in half, emptying the tobacco crumbs on the floorboards between us, spreading them in a circle on the polished wood.

This annoyed me. I was smoking an inexpensive brand of cigarettes. A weekly allowance supplied exactly the amount of coffee, cigarettes, beer, or food I planned to consume weekly. Coming to this party was already a wild splurge. The malt liquor I normally drank on weekends—its gold labels flaking as the bottle warmed in your hand, leaving your palms gilded with its residue—was so cheap that I knew it might offend our host. The broken cigarette on the floor, Isaac explained, was an offering to the Great Spirit he felt impelled to make after seeing my eyes.

From the start, Isaac charmed and annoyed me. He'd borrowed something to make an impressive gesture which left a mess on someone else's floor. He took my phone number. In my junior year, we met for coffee one September night so hot that walking downtown at midnight made us sweat. He'd sprained his ankle trying to jump a train on the tracks along the outer edge of campus, realized he'd lost the keys to his apartment, and limped back to my dormitory, asking for a razor. He had a presentation the next morning. It was long after visiting hours. I brought him a bowl of hot water from the shower. Once he seemed asleep, stretched on the floor by my bed, I grabbed his hand. He held mine to his face. I watched his smile in the yellow streetlight from the window all night.

My roommate was happy for us. "That's what bisexuals do," he explained to his friends. "They lie on the floor all night, holding hands and smiling."

Until Isaac, I'd lied with a patient disarming callousness people found believable but innately incredible. About the house I'd grown up in, places I'd seen, all sorts of things I'd done, letting them soak into my listeners' imaginations, plausible things just skewed from pure truth enough to make them remarkably my own, until, all on their own, they became a digestible whole for myself.

Now I realized, unless I did something drastic, life wasn't going to be nearly as interesting as television, movies or books. I started telling the truth to Isaac, then to his friends and eventually, by accumulated habit, to people in general, because I planned to take him home to my parents. Life and imagination would finally merge, the husks of those separate worlds falling like plaster halves of a bronze mold fresh from a forge, leaving something as real as life and magic as imagination.

Driving home with Isaac, pulling off the highway, passing McMansions and malls, everything was as new for me as it was for him, since I, too, for the past twenty years, had lived somewhere else. I imagined and rejected half a dozen anecdotes. I felt history-less. Honest descriptions felt abstract, more unreal and distant than those faked. Descending the hill, the crunch of the gravel in the driveway sounded like a period. That what I'd previously described of this half-acre plot and its inhabitants actually corresponded to what stood in front of us outweighed any coming-out anxiety.

It was the first time in a long time my parents made eye contact during a meal. My mother: *Is that a boyfriend?* My father: *Must we deal with this tonight?* On the deck, we talked about what Isaac thought of Barcelona, of how it was almost time to start planting fall bulbs. Mom came out to the driveway with cake slices in Saran Wrap, foisting them on Isaac through the car window. Dad had gone inside to read the newspaper. We drove back to campus in silence.

Isaac left me twice. Once temporarily, then for good. First on a weekend house-sit at a professor's house. A long dark drive tread two miles of dirt and rock through towering blackberries to a lake. The drive was mined with cats. Ominous cats. Salutatory cats. We didn't know which. The professor's significant number of cats was the reason we'd been invited to house-sit. A white cat jumped into the drive just before we reached the house, to sit still as a stone. I'd never been given to any particular sympathy toward cats. This one stared us down, fleeing only once it realized I wasn't stopping. Others tore off into the blackberries. The house rose above the trees, a lighted wall of curving glass with framed pictures and quite a lot of what appeared, even at a distance, to be macramé. My headlights shone on the lake. Frost lay over the dead leaves. The door was unlocked. Several hungry cats, recognizable from among those involved in the disturbance on the road, roamed the kitchen. Climbing the stairs, turning on the lights, we began breaking up. The problem was that I smoked and he'd been with someone else. Then it was everything else until, by the end of the weekend, each of us hated the other's face.

It began again as if nothing had gone wrong. A postcard from New York. My apartment's screen door slammed. His eyes fixed on mine until everything of myself sifted out. "I have something to show you," he said, holding my hand, reaching to pull up his shirt, rubbing my hand over the ribs and flesh below his collarbone. "There was a club," he explained, "Inside a cathedral." From there the story went from a church full of shirtless boys to a drug store razor, a sink in Brooklyn, probably still clogged with his chest hair as he spoke. Traces of stubble at my cheek, I thought, in a round, summary way: that was him all over, his chest hair grown out to stubble on the road home, while the rest, miles away, clogged someone else's sink in Brooklyn. And that was me all over, seeing everything his narrative left out.

At the end of my senior year, scuffing my shoe at my parents' deck, it hadn't struck me that I might expect gainful employment from the experience of staying at college all those months and years. I wanted some of what had been kicked out of me in those four years—rushed, with the eyes of other rushed men and women on me, afraid of falling behind, of ending up with no one beneath us.

My plan was to apply to graduate school. Or get to anywhere really. But the thought of student loans left me paralyzed, so it didn't take much to convince me to drive off the night after graduation with Isaac for Seattle. It was simpler than tests or interviews. What's simplest always seems most romantic.

Mountains loomed in the night sky, lifting the car. We crossed the Mississippi at sunrise, Arkansas's green giving way to yellow, glowing in a rainstorm. Oklahoman drivers lifted single fingers from their wheels in greeting. We camped above Santa Fe. In Wyoming, purple hills followed the car windows as if trying to keep up. I slept through Montana, eyes opening to moonlit Idaho. Apples hung from trees by the side of the road, dandelion puffs large and round as human heads. Sporadic bunches of evergreens stood on hills at sunrise. We wound through mountains thick with them. I rolled the window down, breathing.

This is where I would have begun this story, if my

own fake history had nothing to do with the rest of it. As a twenty-two-year-old in a dented hatchback speeding over the Columbia River, putting his window down, wakes to an odor he thinks is a scent, but is ionized molecules of glacier water smashed against rock, bouncing up with explosive force through the evergreens. Breathing air fresher and stronger than anything he's ever inhaled, he might be forgiven for thinking he's somehow driven into the world of his own imagination.

In retrospect, I should have stuck to truth in life. Saved lies for fiction. Instead I find myself writing the truth about lying. This records what happened, from the time the car burrowed into the wet hemlock of the west side of the Columbia, till I recrossed it in a plane headed the other direction.

SEATTLE

Pulling off the highway through crowds and busses, oblivious to everything but the sunset over Puget Sound's mountains, we drove around skyscrapers' bases till the harbor's fog lapped up, smothering the windshield. We boarded a ferry for Cape Flattery, walking swollen planks toward the continental United States' westernmost point, looking out at the ocean. We'd gotten as far as anyone could expect in a car already making unsettling noises pulling into the parking lot. The engine ran long enough to get us back to Seattle. It died halfway up Capitol Hill. We pushed it into a side street.

There are places in our world inspiring a loneliness that seems to come right out of the ground itself. Go out to the bay of a northwestern town. Shout something. You'll see what I mean right away. With the mountains hanging over the water through the fog, that compressed green line on the water's horizon that's really island cedars on the other side, you have the uncanny sense your words are being eaten into by the air and space itself. The land here is so big it swallows things whole. In Seattle this sensation takes you by surprise. Mornings, you bike through the public market, past cheap clapboard pine the colors of a faded super-8 home movie, fog from the bay rising suddenly like the padded damper over a piano's strings, crossing the market, heading up the hill. The ferries cut their lights as the sun rises, invisible, till you pick them out again on the glazed bay.

Wide western streets. The sheer volume of air between things dampens sound, given so much prominence. A silence it takes a while to discover isn't an absence of noise or feeling, but a natural state. Nothing you can do will bring the mountains on the horizon closer, or narrow those wide western streets, lessen the gaping distance between things. Those first days, between stints of realtors' appointments and job interviews, looking for places to sleep at night and things to do in the day, I spent afternoons stretched out in the back of the car, watching accumulated drops of mist roll across the rear windshield.

The Olympics are the furthest point on the horizon you see looking west from downtown on a clear day. On their northern side, Hurricane Ridge, there's a parking lot where kids stand around posing, smoking joints before snowboarding, and a wooden shelter with a plaster model of the ridge and the rest of the Olympics. It's nice to be in a place and to have it spread in front of you as a map at the same time, whole. I wished life had a model like that, so you could look at it whole while being in the middle of it. The mountains make a different impression when viewed from the city. Their silhouette is as familiar to Seattleites as the outline of your house or your car or a grandparent's face—something you couldn't sketch from memory with any accuracy, but with features indelibly engraved in your mind.

The first people who lived here had stories about the mountain range. None of the Indians I met hanging around the pergola in Pioneer Square or along the piers by the ferry terminal could explain the details. But they all knew the mountains once walked and spoke, had adventures and loves and conquests and tragedies before freezing into stone and ice. There's not much else to know about history in this part of the world. Around 1750, a few Spanish sailors roamed the cliffs, stood on the decks of ships looking into the thousand year old spruces, probably got rained on, then turned around and headed back to San Diego.

Certain spots on the planet inspire a kind of inhuman loneliness, so if I felt alone in Seattle, it wasn't for what happened to me there, but empathy for a place most alone of all other spots, stuck up in a far corner of the country even Lewis and Clark never got to. You reach the last leg of a nation's journey in Seattle. Manifest Destiny, stretching its grizzled arm across the continent, reaches for a demitasse of soymilk and another biscotti, turning back to sneer at its own muddy tracks. If this isn't the promised land, then our whole history was one huge folly, from beginning to end.

We rented a two-room apartment off Broadway for $460 a month, living on humus and coffee. Isaac kept both rooms filled with the smoke from Nag Champa incense from midnight to two a.m. At two-fifteen, the lights blinked off in the bookstore across the street's plate glass, after which the bookstore's night salesclerk turned off the shop's bubble machine, pausing outside to lock the door and light a joint on the sidewalk, then strode lazily toward the undimmed lights of Broadway. Once the two-thirty bus glided down the hill a few yards from the window, sparks shooting from its electric cable, we brushed our teeth and went to bed. We worked afternoons serving things like crème brulée and flavored tortellini to lawyers on the fifty-second floor of a skyscraper. We brought leftovers home for dinner and breakfast. Our mouths had the constant tang of balsamic vinegar, arugula and feta. He played his guitar in cafes mostly, or in parks, and I wrote, hunched in a corner of the floor over a laptop.

That first year in the Northwest I read a lot about Microsoft and developed a tolerance for double lattes (or double Americanos, when times weren't as good). We learned to order coffee drinks, and once our money ran out we learned to make them, measuring out doses of black grounds so fine they felt like velvet between our fingers, working their way gradually into the fibers of all our clothes. I walked around with the smell of roasted coffee coming out my pores in a city that is in a daily process of inventing itself, creating its own culture, and at night sometimes found the webbing between my fingers still sticky with milk and cream and honey.

The second year I realized I wasn't impervious to a peculiar brand of northwestern mold spores that seemed in and of themselves to drive a good number of my friends to Taos or Austin and caused me to run out and buy protein deposit removal tablets for my extended wear contacts for the first time in years. There was supposed to be a recession on in the early 90s. Young America out of work. We were confused, yet savvy, or nihilistic, or something. A series of contemporary films was depicting a generation as likely to die vomiting of a heroin overdose in the corporate restroom as to take that tree-planting sabbatical in Kenya they'd been talking about by the office water cooler. The people we met did things like reading tarot cards in cafes or pulling coffee shots or delivering packages on bikes.

We never had toilet paper. We went around the corner to the coffee house, keeping our books on shelves of cinderblocks and boards, suggesting to each other that a lack of material possessions was a small price to pay for having moved three thousand miles, placating ourselves by becoming Buddhists, attending group meditations at the Mahayana center on Pike Street. We wanted to move downtown. We wanted to move to the country. We wanted to move to San Francisco. We spent a lot of time looking at the Space Needle. We waited for the imminent Republican backlash that would take place after Clinton's first term, swearing we'd pack for Amsterdam. In a city far from everything, local problems represented situations of enormous moral scope like elongated shadows in the evening sun or early morning. Every month he came up short on rent, going to cafes instead of eating at home, wondering how it happened.

At the library, I looked up old *Times* photos, printing them from microfilm to hang on the refrigerator—grainy images of rubble, crushed cars, downtown blocks ruined by earthquakes of '49 and '65. I convinced myself I had writer's block. Witnessing an earthquake might relieve it. I took better drugs than had been available where we'd come from, had amazing clarity and peace, writing magic sentence fragments full of meaning and fervor. Looking outside at the rain, sleeping and waking, I forced my dreams into words.

No one I knew had lived in Seattle long enough to live through an earthquake. I don't know why I'd been waiting for one in particular. The earth moves all over the place every day. Our solar system is an aerobics classroom. Things spin, bounce, collide, scream off alone leaving trails of light. The moon stretches tides the way you stretch a strand of bubble gum. Earthquakes are just two parties locked in each other's arms, each headed in different directions. Most of the time they inch toward spaces they desire without conflict. The earthquake starts when each side's own movement becomes more powerful that what holds them together. It ends when each finds a new place to rest, shoulder to shoulder, locked in that same embrace, this time with a new companion.

I was tense in cafes when they cranked up the speakers, the bass rumbling the floorboards. One afternoon in Café Paradiso I found myself clutching the seat of my chair, looking covertly around the room for confirmation of anyone else feeling the tremors. In a split second of uncertain panic, I'd locked eyes with a guy at another table as our saucers and cups jarred on each table's surface, each of us not knowing, just for that second, whether to be scared or to smile. Uncertainly, we held our gaze a second longer than human nature or politeness normally permits, till each of us was sure. Then we looked away again, I to my book, he to his newspaper, his form fading into the rest of the room in my peripheral vision, his eyes burned into my own eyelids like blinking after staring at the sun.

You can only describe an earthquake by describing

the objects it affects. It hits your stomach, giving you a dizzy spell. You try to recall what you had for lunch, have an urge to lie down. You watch the picture swaying on the wall, hear the chatter of silverware in a drawer, and glasses on their shelves ring from something in a hypocenter fifty miles below, where two things, once locked together, split, each following some inner movement stronger than their bond.

Todd was a dark scrawny kid, a bicycle courier with an unfinished degree in philosophy, the first in a series Isaac brought home from Café Paradiso. When they closed the bedroom door, making it apparent they weren't coming out until the next morning, I studied the couch, then without really thinking about it, put my shoulder to the door and broke the lock. They didn't say anything. Todd fiddled with the undone strap of his overalls. I excused myself and went for a walk.

He showed up at the door while Isaac wasn't home.

"Isaac's not here," I said. Todd warmed up the remains of my morning coffee. Todd wrote poetry. This eventually made things better between us. He started coming over in the afternoons to sit in a ragged armchair I'd picked up in the alley outside the building and talk when Isaac wasn't there. I began not to mind so much. He said that after I left that night he'd scolded Isaac for not going after me. "The next time it happens," Todd said—meaning the next time

Isaac brought someone else home; after a few weeks there had been other times—"you ought to get someone to come over while they're in the other room. So you have someone to talk to. You shouldn't have to leave your own house every time someone comes over. Call somebody. Call anybody you know. Put the phone on speaker. Keep them on the line."

This seemed logical. The only people I knew with a local number were Brandon and Lisa, the couple upstairs who'd let us use their phone for messages when we moved in.

Lisa and Brandon had been married for eight years. They were that deep pale color that comes from zero sun exposure. They evidently cut each other's hair. Sometimes the results were good, other times one was tempted to suspect the involvement of malice. For the first years of their marriage Lisa had worked while Brandon put himself through school. During the latter years, Brandon worked while Lisa housewifed. Now, Lisa was reporting for duty at the neighborhood Kinko's. Brandon had been fired from the university's photo lab, deciding to spend his surplus free time in the pursuit of his long-underdeveloped bisexuality—for Lisa, unfortunately, an experience Seattle afforded more easily than their native Montgomery had. As Brandon's adventures extended, Lisa began having breakdowns, then started an affair herself to square things off. I gave them serious slack because once, at one of their parties after a strident argument with Isaac in our own apartment, I'd asked if they'd heard us shouting. They'd looked at each other for a minute, searching each others' eyes before saying "No" together, in unison, so kindly and reassuringly that I believed them until I heard their own voices tearing into each other quite clearly one morning a week later. Tom Waits droned above our ceiling from their apartment most evenings, a blur of angry voices cutting below the gruff bass. Lisa and Brandon fought in their room, coming out once they'd made up, smiling with some new plan, which usually involved going to the cafe around the corner or shopping in the leather boutique on Broadway.

Isaac's normal one night stand involved bringing someone home and introducing me as "a friend." Isaac strummed his guitar at irregular intervals, till the voices dropped in the other room. The light went out. Then silence. Then noises. The problem was the noises. The walls were thin. By nine o'clock one Monday night the lights were already out. I called Lisa and Brandon. Brandon answered the phone.

"Hey, Brandon, how's it going?" I said.

"Hey."

"This is Ian, downstairs Ian."

"Fine."

"I just thought I'd call and say thanks, we finally got a phone. How's things upstairs?"

"Shitty. Have you seen Lisa? Lisa disappeared again."

"Disappeared?"

"Same story. Two days. No news."

"What are you going to do?"

"Change the lock is what I ought to do. You haven't seen her by any chance?"

"No . . . " The sex noises starting early, I would have appreciated a television.

"What are you yelling for, man?" he was saying. "I can hear you fine."

"Isaac has someone over," I said, louder.

"Well, damn, son, you're hurting my ear."

"Sorry."

"Okay, well, look—you know me and Lisa were going to Belize. Take pictures, finally get a decent portfolio together. I just don't think it's meant to happen. Maybe I'll just go do some hiking by myself."

"You're not worried about her?"

"In general, yes. But she wasn't that crazy about Belize anyway. So what's your weird thing that's going on?"

The sex noises had hesitantly resumed.

"It's a boyfriend problem."

"Is he missing?"

"No, he's here. With someone else."

"So it's an extramarital problem?"

"Like that." On the other side of the wall the mattress springs gave.

"Kick him out, dude. You don't need that kind of craziness. Listen, if you see Lisa tell her not to touch my stuff. Just tell her, okay? Any idea what the weather down there's like this time of year?"

"Pack extra socks."

"Take care of yourself. Thanks for calling. And get rid of that guy. You don't need that shit."

I stood on the porch. The front door opened and the boy from inside stepped out with a sheepish backward smile in my direction. I figured this would be a good time to get some sleep.

I had an excuse to call upstairs after Isaac's door closed two nights later. Brandon answered the phone.

"Hey, did Lisa show up?" I said.

"Yeah, finally. Guess where she was hiding the last three days."

"Where?"

"At the neighbor's. On the other side of this fucking wall."

"And she didn't call?"

"They took some kind of animal tranquilizers. She said she couldn't find the phone."

"So she's okay?"

"I'm out of here," he said, yelling away from the phone. In the background was a sound like something breaking.

"You're going to Belize?"

"Damn straight. I've had enough of this shit."

A click. A door slammed upstairs. Tom Waits thumped through my ceiling. I went out for a walk. From outside, you could see someone pacing at the curtainless windows of the second floor.

GREEN LIGHT, 7-11

I drove to Portland to spend some time alone on the road, letting the car roll down the slope of the Nisqually valley to the stagnant green base of Puget Sound, rain pouring steadily off truckers' tires onto the windshield. The leaves were that first green of the year, when they've only seen the sun for a couple of days. I always want to push April, hurry it, never really accept it as a real month, just a spacious wet gap between March and May.

Things are however you look at them, I decided. A relationship depends on who needs whom most. As if there's some trick in the DNA, an indention in a gene's surface filling with some chemical produced by a lover's proximity, feeling pain when its indention is left empty again. In the beginning both parties hem and haw and vie back and forth, each trying to figure it out—who loves more, will put up with more to be loved. There are rare, blunt moments when each sees it quite clearly. But an indention is an indention, filled or not. Like mirror neurons—that twinge of reception in a fiber to a fiber in another's brain, two separate sets of tissue, reaching toward each other from behind two separate skulls, reaching at the empty space between them. This whole last two years had been some kind of bliss Isaac decided to spoil. But that wasn't exactly true, and looking at it that way wasn't helping.

I was carded for cigarettes in a nameless cedar town. Portland came up—a widening highway, splashes of suburbs, bridges. Brandon had loaned me a car, giving me the number of a friend who had mushrooms. After taking orders from people in the building, I had enough for food and the trip there and back. I sat outside a bookstore drinking coffee, wishing I could remember the dream I'd had the night before, then took off through downtown along the river.

At my mother's insistence, I was having dinner with the Smarts in Lake Oswego at 6:30. After which I could call a number to get the mushrooms. My mother had been trying to get me to call the Smarts for months. Her last words in any recent phone conversations ran, "Why don't you give Andrew and Lois a call if you're going to stay all the way over there?" And here I was in Oregon.

Andrew, Lois and I sat around a table in the upper level of the Taste of China. Lois, just off the plane from San Jose delivering employee review scores to a district office, guarded her watch closely to be in time for a city councilpersons' meeting. Lois was chairwoman of the library committee, and Lake Oswego's citizens wanted a more computer-friendly building. Andrew poured tea. We all ordered asparagus. We discussed CD-ROM. In

1993, people spoke of CD-ROM in the singular, as a concept. Technology came in capital letters like government agencies or chemical compounds. At the end of the meal, Lois confided a growing passion for vampire novels. I mentioned Anne Rice. Lois rolled her eyes. We made our way toward the door. Andrew, ambivalent toward his wife's recently increasing interest in the living dead, asked a million times for me to stay the night in Lake Oswego. Making excuses, I followed Andrew's Volvo to the highway, then took off through downtown along the river to a phone booth to call Brandon's friend.

A girl's voice answered. "What? Oh, you're a friend of Brandon and Lisa? Hey. How's Brandon and Lisa these days? Okay, let me give you some sort of directions." I followed her sort of directions to an apartment block across the river. There was a party going on on the floor below hers. The building's window frames shook with the beat of soundless bass. The hall was full of a nervous energy. Her door opened. Three curious feline heads appeared at the bottom. The cats made a struggle for the hall. The girl pulled them back with a foot, laughing. I slipped inside. She slammed the door behind us.

She couldn't have been more than sixteen, with acne and glasses. She and her boyfriend were eating dinner on plates held on their laps in the living room. Cats hovered. "I couldn't get mushrooms," she laughed. "But," she said, reaching under the sofa, "I've got . . . pot! Smoke all you want. Take the rest with you." She lit a pipe, but their domesticity, the two of them, eating dinner from their laps, made me want to get home again. I gave her my neighbors' money and left them to their dinner.

Near Olympia I stopped at a gas station with a dining room and pulled out my laptop. The gray-bearded cook at the counter shifted a pen behind his ear, watching. "What kind of a contraption is that?" he asked.

"It's a computer," I said.

"What are you writing?"

"A book."

"What about?"

"About my life."

"Well," he said. "That might be a nice book if you've got an interesting life."

"Oh, no," I said, sitting at a gas station restaurant in the middle of nowhere, past midnight on a Friday.

"Shoot." He smiled, stepping back to the counter. I could tell if I turned my head he'd start talking again. I wanted to be writing, so I stared at the screen, tapping the shift keys. I wrote about dinner with the Smarts and the girl with the cats, telling myself the important thing was to get the facts straight. Then I remembered I wanted to be writing fiction. For the first time, with surprise, I noticed the discrepancy.

The manager wandered into the dining room. "You're stealing our electricity," she said flatly.

Outside, I smoked. The stars were out. It was fairly warm. I called Isaac. At the end of the conversation, under the trees by the phone booth, I said "I love you," just to see if he said it back.

"Great!" he said. "Drive safe!"

I realized I didn't even vaguely miss him. I curled up in the back of the car, dreaming of being a child again, of stuffing pillows under our clothes and slam dancing to the Dead Kennedys any time they left us alone in the house with a babysitter.

Pulling out of the parking lot at dawn, I was stopped by a police car for not signaling. I pulled my seatbelt on before the policeman came to the window. I didn't have more than ten dollars in the bank, and wondered how I was going to pay for whatever it was he was going to charge me for. He said he was giving me a warning. I watched the policeman's fingers at the edge of the window, his mouth asking if I had insurance. I reached into the glove compartment and started a slow, methodical search through it, expecting that if I looked thoroughly enough, insurance would magically appear. I found the title and registration, an instruction manual, a screwdriver, a stick of gum. The policeman gave me an address and a special ticket for people who think they probably have insurance but forget to keep it in their glove compartments. I was too nervous about the policeman to think about the pot.

I pulled over at a state park to stop for a while to hike, the ground so wet that the earth seemed to have been laid over water. Leave a footprint, and water pools slowly into it from all sides.

At home, I spent an hour looking at old photographs. Isaac playing guitar on a sidewalk, sitting on a porch swing, standing proud over a vegetable garden. I wanted to say to his face, *I would have done anything for you.* But I was in an apartment in a marginal neighborhood thinking about a face which didn't really exist anymore. He came home, full of coffee, bouncing off the walls, alone, and lay under me, my palm pressed to the back of his neck, his curls between my fingers. The lights off, I still knew the exact color of his skin, a hand pressed to the muscles of his back.

He got up. Still napping when he came in again, glad to see his head in the door, I saw from his face there was someone with him. I got up to make coffee. Now that Brandon was gone, I was out of numbers to call. But I owed his wife her pot, so I called upstairs on the off-chance of getting her, wishing I could have brought the phone into the warm kitchen, where the coffee was going. It wasn't cordless. I stood in the living room leaning on the window sill, the phone in my hand, looking out at the bus cables, feeling the cold radiating in from the glass, with Isaac's door behind me.

"Hello," Lisa said.

"Hi, Lisa?"

"Speaking."

"It's Ian, downstairs."

"Who? Oh. The folks with the sex noises. You know, this place has one hell of a thin floor. If you'll excuse my saying so. I've been drinking."

"It's not me."

"Yeah, okay."

"Um, I got back from Portland today."

"Successfully?"

"Relatively."

"I'll come down. My apartment's kind of a mess."

"Ok."

There was a thump from the bedroom door behind me.

"You sure you're not busy?"

"No."

"Be there in a second."

There were serious noises coming from the other side of the wall by the time Lisa knocked half an hour later, in a bathrobe and tennis shoes.

"Actually you caught me at a good time," she said, dreadlocks tied in a tight bun. She was prettier without makeup. "For mushrooms. I was just settling in for a nice quiet orgy of self-pity." Lisa sat down, extending a bottle of vodka as more muffled sounds came from the other side of the wall. "Well, it isn't you after all," she said. Another muffled gasp came from behind the door. "Go on!" Lisa said, beating a fist on the wall. "Don't mind us! Carpe Diem! That's your boyfriend, I take it? Or are you running some kind of business?"

"He has somebody over," I said. "And I have some bad news."

"They're having some good news. Maybe it'll even out the ch'i in your apartment."

"Actually your friend in Portland only had pot."

"That works." A scraping sound came from the bedroom, then a bang as the headboard hit the wall. Lisa gazed at the door. "I take it this is some pretty potent stuff."

Shoving it into the folds of her bathrobe, she rolled a joint, leaning back as I took a swig of her vodka. "So," she said, exhaling slowly. "I guess you guys have a pretty easy-going relationship. That never really worked for me."

I frowned.

"Seems like you're pretty cool about it," she said. "I mean, you're not the jealous type, I take it."

"Who isn't?"

"At least he didn't move to Belize." She looked out the window as the noises subsided. "What are you going to *do*?"

"I don't know."

"Are you staying?"

"In the apartment?"

"In *Seattle*. You ought to move out of this apartment. Move into mine. We'll save tons of money. I'd move into yours, but I'm already *living* in mine."

"All right."

"Good," Lisa said, taking the bottle, standing to go.

I stood on the front stoop for a while. The evening's boy came out and went down the steps. Isaac sat on the bed with the door open, the light on. I didn't say anything. He didn't say anything. He sauntered stiffly to the kitchen, gazing into the refrigerator. "Who was that you were talking to?" he asked.

"Lisa. Upstairs."

Pulling himself up on the counter beside me, he traced a finger across the seam of my jeans. "Baby." He leaned closer. "Are you okay?"

"Fine." I couldn't look at him, then did anyway. His eyes, timid, blue, were waiting to be looked at.

"Look," he said. "I was thinking. Maybe we need some time apart."

"Fine."

"I might move in with somebody next month." He put his face, twisted and red and angry, close to mine and didn't say anything for a minute. "Do you think that would be a good idea?"

"Yeah. A fine idea."

I'm over-fastidious about the state of my soul. But

there are moments when you know you're about to be scarred, and can only watch it happen. Incidents you know, even as they happen, are going to leave a nasty impression. Once during a car crash, in the passenger seat watching the side of a tractor trailer come in through the window, I was thinking the same thing. Another time, on a school biology trip to a medical lab, we were shown the severed torso of a woman, with seared flesh around the waist and the legs. There's nothing you can do. Both times I simply thought, *This is going to leave a mark*, ruminating on the pity of it. And they did. I'm never entirely comfortable on a highway in the rain. I'm never comfortable with that part of a woman's body. And, after that night, I didn't want to look at Isaac—or for a while, anyone—in the eyes again.

Lisa began leaving note cards with recipes taped to our door.

Quick 'N Easy Recipe #1
Beer

Open a beer and drink it.

Open another beer and drink it.

Open another beer and drink it.

Maybe have some food, something really disgusting like overdone Ramen, that you don't actually eat more than two bites of.

Drink another beer.

Go buy some more beer and drink it.

Call an ex-lover to tell him how much you really cared about him. Don't say it straight out. Beat around the bush for about an hour, long-distance, then don't actually ever say it, but say somthing sarcastic instead and try to get him to hang up on you, while drinking some more beer.

Stay at home until you fall asleep listening to Depeche Mode.

If you're still having fun, go back to the grocery store and get more beer. Try not to sway back and forth at the check-out counter. Spend a lot of time wondering if the clerks realize you're drunk and/or care.

Smirk when they card you. Look at the rows of gum behind you. Enjoy the fluorescent lights. Wonder if the one other shopper in the store notices the muzak as much as you do. Realize the muzak is definitely a soundtrack to your life in particular, if you think about it, and this particular song is a strong statement about your life right now. Try to remember that, so when you walk through the parking lot you'll still have it in your head. The last beers are always the loneliest. Turn out the lights. Drink them in the dark, listening to traffic. Finish with cigarettes and aspirin.

And this:

Quick 'N Easy Recipe #2
Pasta with Bleu Cheeze

Basil

Pasta

Red Pepper flakes

garlic

Bleu Cheeze

olive oil

Fresh Mozzarella

Get that cool kind of multicolored pasta with all kinds of shapes – at the Seattle Co-Op they call it Wizard's Delight or something inane like that. The more spirals and weird trumpet-shapes, the more the Cheeze will get caught in the little frills and stick there, like it's supposed to.

Boil the pasta until it's like, almost totally al dente.

Meanwhile, chop up some garlic really fine, like two or three large cloves per serving, and dice the basil fine and make a little pile of them on the cutting board so they keep all their juice together.

Crumble the bleu cheeze into about 3 table-spoons worth. When the pasta is done and draining, fry the garlic in a little frying pan with 2 tablespoons of oil. Throw in the red pepper flakes. Put the basil and crumbled cheeze on the pasta in the serving dish. When the garlic is cooked, pour the oil over the pasta. This will melt the Cheeze and wilt the Basil.

Mix it all very well, so the garlicky cheeze and the basil get into all the crevices of the pasta. Slice the mozzarella into ½ inch thick pieces, eat them, but leave one on top of the dish, in the middle, with a little piece of basil on it and another shake of red pepper. Looks very impressive. Drink wine, go to bed.

What could be easier? Mmmm.

BUT HE SWORE THAT HE DIDN'T HAVE A GUN

The week I moved into Lisa's place, they found Kurt Cobain dead in Madrona. It was raining. On Broadway people you barely knew would come up to you on the sidewalk, pulling you under storefront awnings to tell you the position of the body. Face up, with the rifle at his side, was the story for the first part of the day. Then face down, with the gun in his hand. Isaac went to the memorial service to comfort bereaved teenagers. Though Cobain was ostensibly straight, when an interview in a local magazine Isaac had left behind asked what he would most like to be doing at the moment of the interview, his response was, "I'd rather be tricking on the streets of Seattle."

Lisa disappeared, leaving another recipe pasted to the refrigerator.

Quick 'N Easy Recipe #3
Marijuana

You will need:

a bowl

a beach

a hip but quiet person, or a very mellow dog

Drive to the beach. Lean down in the seat to pack the bowl. Smoke it with the visors down, freaking every time someone comes within 20 feet of the car. Roll the windows down. People say you get more stoned by leaving them up, but it's not worth it. Sit in the seat a long time because it's comfortable and you don't know if you're ready to deal with the world yet. Talk to your person/dog, etc.

Get out of the car. Make sure you have your keys, water, lighter, person/dog, etc. Close the door. Lock it.

Walk on the beach.

Smile. Ignore annoying children. Make your person/dog realize it's quiet time by being noncommittally silent. Feel the wind. Take your shoes off, tying the laces together and strapping them over your shoulder. Or have the person/dog carry them. Chase birds. Lie down. Close your eyes. Dissolve. Wake up two hours later sandy and wonderful.

Drive home, clean the apartment and listen to U2.

Brandon had been working as a bike courier. Lisa suggested I give that a try.

My first day of employment as a bike courier, I had

four flat tires. I started off to work late, making up time going down Pike Street, listening to a tape with a song called "Baby baby baby bitch," thinking of Isaac. The song got stuck in my head, especially the one line, "Fuck you, you stinking asshole," my favorite. I got to work on time and got my radio and jersey, but nobody was at the counter assigning bikes. The bikes on the rack were clunky things with big wire baskets, so I cruised out of the base on my own bike. It was an hour before my first flat tire, not too far from base. I was calling in, "03 to base."

"Base here."

"I've got a flat. I'll be a minute getting in."

"10-4." Flat tire one.

I got in, got a lecture about taking my own bike out, and Stew—more on Stew later—gave me a bike assignment. Number 34.

I headed out the door with Number 34. Another courier on his way in said, "Dude! You got the cool bike."

I looked at Number 34. It didn't look like a cool bike, even by company standards, but: nice frame, new bar ends, fresh brakes. I figured Stew liked me. I pumped up the rear tire a little. I headed to my next drop.

A word about Stew, and about bicycle couriers in general. A bicycle courier is vain, to begin with. He sees every recptionist[1] in every office fawn over his thighs and mussed hair. He imagines every pinstripe-suited yuppie in every elevator, frowning at his goatee, secretly envies his bicycle courier freedom. This, combined with a near-constant adrenaline buzz, short attention span fueled by the habit of movement, and spending a good part of his day staring down at his own legs, feeds his bravado. Todd, the tights-wearing, loogie-hocking, stubble-growing shuttle courier I traded packages off with was enormously fond, during the odd leisure moment shared outside office towers, of boasting of his biking exploits in abridged blips. "Yeah," he'd say to me, out of the blue before pedaling off, "I once did Harbor Island and back on a thirty minute rush." He smiles and rides away, admirably maneuvering through traffic while eating a peanut butter and jelly sandwich. It made my heart pound.

Most of us hadn't been there long. We didn't stay long. Reasons for retirement typically involved going back to school. Said grounds were elaborated slightly, but served all purposes. Whether you wanted to visit you girlfriend in San Diego or felt a drinking binge coming on, you said "I'm going back to school" with a straight face. They let you off for a while, never surprised when you showed up again two weeks later. They had a soft spot for higher education. Or they'd forgotten your face by then.

---

[1] Or "deceptionist," according to Stew.

Stew stood out, pudgy by courier standards. Stew only biked in emergencies. The rest of the time he fixed brakes and installed radiators in the cars. He had a shop at the back of the base with a poster of three girls in bikinis sitting on the hood of a Camaro.

Stew gave out jerseys in the morning. He'd been intent on a checklist when I'd come up for my shirt. I waited until he was done. Without looking up from his clipboard, Stew guffed out, "My telepathic powers are low today, so why don't you just tell me what the fuck you want?" I made my way out. He'd looked after me a little sheepishly. I figured that was why Stew had given me Number 34, the coolest bike on the rack.

Number 34 lasted from the Westlake Mall to the Art Museum before the air I'd pumped into its back tire hissed out through a slow leak. I called in again, waiting for somebody with a less cool bike to come pick up my packages so I could hobble back to base. Flat tire two.

Back at base I asked Stew if he could help me fix my own tire and he said yeah, maybe. Which was nice. At the end of the day, he showed me how to feel around inside the tire with a finger to look for pieces of glass. It was simple. Sand the tube, glue the patch, force out the air, wait for it to dry. We worked quietly side by side, surrounded by tools and bike innards. It didn't cross my mind that Stew was probably the one who had patched 34 in the first place. So I pumped the tire and thanked him, starting home, heading for the ATM and the liquor store. By the time I got to the liquor store the tire was flaccid. Flat tire three.

I cursed, trudging five blocks to the shop where I'd bought the bike, swigging a bottle of Popov. I bought a new tube, put it in, and biked home. Almost. Just blocks from the apartment, my fourth tire of the day gave up the ghost. I had to walk her. Lisa sat on the front porch with a family-sized bucket of Kentucky Fried Chicken. We split what was left of the vodka.

A few weeks later, delivering a package to a law firm, I locked eyes with those same eyes I'd stared at during my imagined earthquake in Café Paradiso, standing by the receptionist's counter, attached to a suit. "For Mark King," I said, sliding the package to the receptionist. The man with the eyes at the counter intercepted it before she reached for it.

"I can take that to him," he said. "I'm going right in." He smiled a smile that was more than a smile, less than a facial gesture, formulaic as a signal, palpable as if he'd just reached out to touch my shoulder.

The receptionist signed my file. I turned to go. But something strange had happened. Like Nietzsche hearing Wagner, I was nauseous.

Quick 'N Easy Recipe #4
Blue Lagoon Soup

1 gallon Corn Syrup

3 bottles blue food coloring

5 tbsp. Whole Jamaican Allspice

Malibu Barbie

Malibu Ken

several inflated condoms

Quick 'N Easy Recipe #5
Jabba's Cake

200 Tootsie Rolls

1 cup flour

1 cup corn syrup

¼ cup Tylenol 3 with codeine

Jabba the Hutt Action Figure

greased cake pan

3 cups Crisco

Dexatrim

Frosting:

    10 tubes Wintergreen ChapStick

    ½ cup green jelly worms

½ cup cocoa

1 cup corn syrup

1 package instant chocolate pudding

Root beer

Sift the flour. Mix with the corn syrup, root beer, Tylenol, Tootsie Rolls and ChapStick.

Pour into a cake mold.

Bake at 350 degrees for two or three or four hours.

Allow to cool.

For frosting, boil ingredients in a double boiler and mix well, chill over ice while stirring smooth.

Place Jabba the Hutt on top with an empty can of root beer.

Sprinkle with Tylenol and Dexatrim.

Harbor Tours

Isaac left behind a map of the city's gay bars. Over a plate of macaroni and cheese one afternoon, I stared at it, then set out walking. The first bar had wood paneling, a bow-tied bartender and two leering businessmen in suits. I ordered a beer. In the second, a small red chamber with a juke box and photographs of nude men in bondage, two men in jeans stood against the bar with hands in each others' pockets while another chain-smoked Capris in a corner. I had another beer.

The third bar was confusingly crowded with glass fish tanks and a sea of men in silk ties. I found myself with one of them in a car headed back down the hill. He'd offered me anything in the world I wanted for dinner. I wanted breakfast. We were sitting at a sidewalk cafe two feet from his illegally-parked car. I was scarfing down two eggs Florentine and a plate of hash browns with the large part of a bottle of ketchup. "You are so cute, so sweet, so butch," he was saying, smiling a row of perfect teeth. He was a chef from Columbia, with eleven brothers and sisters. He wasn't eating anything. He was enunciating. "Ah want to sock your deek. Ah waaant to sick your deeek." Until he repeated himself I thought he was speaking Spanish.

I didn't want him to sock my deeek.

"Ah, who cares?" he said. We went on joking. I said I had to go to the bathroom. The urinal was one of those kinds like a porcelain trough filled with ice so men could amuse themselves melting it in patterns with their piss. I amused myself this way. Out on the sidewalk, I turned under the trees and around the back of the block.

As I opened our building's door, there were stomping boots in the stairwell. Lisa's image spun down from the top of the stairs. She was wearing a leopard skin pillbox hat. I tried to remember what it was I was supposed to tell her.

"Fucked up?" she asked, cocking her head to one side and looking me in the eye.

"I think so."

"Well, come with, then," she said. "Let's go."

A car sat running outside at the curb, with another couple in the front seat. We got in, Lisa made introductions, the music was turned up, the car started toward Broadway. I leaned back, staring up at the ceiling. "You aren't going to be sick, are you?" Lisa asked confidentially.

"No, I'm never sick."

"That must be nice. I'd like to try it some time." The lights outside the windows left her face a blur. She pulled a can of Sapporo from her coat and handed it to me. "How's Isaac?"

"I haven't seen him."

"He was a freak."

"Kind of," I said.

"Is he really going to Scotland?"

"He's been saying that all year."

"I bet he'll go," she said. "I bet he'll go and be the biggest, craziest thing they've ever seen in Scotland." Taking the can back, she took a long sip. The car drove on, shot through with neon, then dark. "At least he didn't go to Belize," she said, looking out the window.

The car circled an intersection. We came to a stop in front of Gasworks Park. Lisa pulled my arm. We ran in the dark, feet blurred beneath us on the grass, rolling down a hill, arms to our sides, stars and earth spinning one after the other. When I sat up near the bottom and looked up, the sky quivered, the stars still and the blackness around them vibrating. The others lay on the grass beside us, screaming with laughter.

Quick 'N Easy Recipe #6
Magic Pancakes

3 boxes Kraft Macaroni 'n Cheeze

2 8-oz. cans creamed corn

1 8-oz. can of Pork 'n Beans

nutmeg

3 crayons, paper removed (any color)

bong water

mashed Altoids

Stir the ingredients over medium heat in a saucepan until crayons are melted and macaroni is al dente.

Drain excess water.

Pour into pancake shapes and fry in olive oil.

Serve with honey and more melted crayons.
Serves 12–15.

At first Isaac only moved five blocks away. I wouldn't go near his house, but sometimes rode past it, coming home or going to work. Its windows, green shutters and the mouth of its porch were like an empty face.

I told the bike courier people I was going back to school, sent out a dozen resumes, took the ferry to Vashon Island, lived on pancakes, orange juice and generic cigarettes in a youth hostel for a week, then took the ferry home and listened to my voicemail. I found myself wanting to talk. A message from the Seattle Harbor Tours' director suggested I might get my chance. As a guide, four daily hours of nonstop monologue was required. I passed a phone interview and took a bus to south Seattle to fill out some forms. With the season's other new guides, I was bussed to Vancouver, so the company could show us how it felt to be tourists for a weekend.

We were driven in a luxury coach, handed envelopes of spending money, and deposited in hotels with the wives of upper-level executives of the company who wanted a weekend away or, as everyone assumed, were sent to spy on us. And with the tour guides. Rob, a big guy with a perm frizzed like a lion's mane, quickly became my smoking friend. The executives' wives smoked. Rob and I spent rest breaks standing on the other side of the bus listening to them.

Melanie was a girl in a leather jacket with jet black bobbed hair in the third seat from the front of the bus.

Matt, who seemed to have as the main feature of his personality the fact that he still lived at home but had worked for the company long enough to carry a beeper, wanted to play cards. When drunk, he asked awkward questions with an expression that hinted he expected you to beat him up after you answered.

Rob was sarcastic to Matt while at the same time making a good show of deferring to his seniority. Matt seemed to enjoy looking for the barb hidden in each of Rob's comments. The rest of the passengers sprawled across velour seats in floral skirts enjoying cassettes of Simon and Garfunkel medleys.

Matt was obsessed with the idea that we should go jogging at six in the morning, so I switched rooms to bunk with Rob, pulling out a cigarette to go to the balcony. "Look, Ian," Rob said, stepping out on the balcony with me. "From here you can see the street." I looked. You could. Rob had the air conditioner running full blast. The room smelled like regurgitated carpet. "Look at all those people down there," Rob said. "Betcha they're going to have a good time tonight. You like to party, dontcha?"

Melanie took us all dancing, listening to Nine Inch Nails in a dark room filled with the haze of a smoke machine while the titles of songs ran in red letters on a screen. It was the first time I was so acutely aware of Canadian drinking habits. Which was simply that they drank exactly as much as people ought to drink, by any self-respecting undergraduate's standards. It rained. The bus took us to a swinging bridge over a gorge. A few of us crossed it. Most of us sat staring gloomily at the bridge's wet planks, rifling the gift shop for ibuprophin. I spent the ride back memorizing interesting historical Seattle facts, lulled to sleep by Rob's snoring at my side.

My first day of work on the tour boat, a woman raised her hand to ask if Seattle wasn't smaller than New York.

Passengers came off cruise ships after a week of moose and glaciers, promised urban excitements. Our job was to report through a speaker what passed at our sides as the boat made hour-long stints back and forth along the edge of the harbor. Matt, after weeks of frustration in explaining downtown to retired groups from small towns, had fine-tuned a "non-informative" tour. *Those are skyscrapers*, he would say into the microphone as the boat drifted along the wharf in its hour-long loop. *They are very very tall buildings. People work in them. In offices.* Or, *That is a restaurant. It exchanges your dollars for edible fish and liquid refreshments.* Or, *To the left is the market, where vendors renting spaces sell various souvenirs and perishable foodstuffs.* Or, *To your right on the warf, you will notice a city bus passing. For a small fee and on a regular schedule, it transports people from one point to another.* When passengers were restless or fog drew a caul over the skyline: *To the side of the deck, you will notice the harbor for which our tour is named. It's wet and cold.* A few times, I felt the temptation to begin making up stories, edging toward my own phrases. I fought it down. I had a memorized list of names, facts and numbers.

With my first paycheck, I bought a yard sale desk and spent nights listening to Lisa's radio, squinting out the window to see what was going on inside the bookstore across the street. Everything I wrote came out sounding like a travel guide.

Life slowed down without Isaac around, taking on my own speed as if I were coming down off some itchy amphetamine. Wanting more, finding the bottle empty, frantic, then learning to enjoy things slowly, remembering the crazy spin of living someone else's life.

I dated haphazardly. It seemed impossible, in a strange city, to date in any methodical way.

Lisa told me, over coffee, relationships only worked because of common interests. "That, and maybe the way people smell. Of course," she said, "Everyone has their own ideal. But that's where things get screwed up. You have to find someone with common interests. And like the way they smell. But you have to get rid of your ideal image. So what's yours?"

"I guess . . . when I was a kid, we had this *Guinness Book of World Records*, and there was this page about Arnold Schwarzenegger."

She gave me a blank look. "See? It doesn't mean you care about—Arnold *Schwarzenegger*?—in life. I used to meet cute boys and it never worked out. I kept falling for crazy people, so I saw a shrink, who said the thing was to find common interests before falling in love."

To be honest, I couldn't think of anything I was really interested in beyond my own thought processes and perceptions. I occasionally found someone who seemed as interested in my own thoughts as myself, but no one's interest in them was as deep as my own. Lisa said I should list my requirements for a boyfriend with three major points. So I made a list. Someone I wouldn't lie to. Speak at least two languages. Have access to a working car. Ideally, get my literary references.

Boyfriend one was a social worker from New Mexico, who spoke Spanish and owned a car. I met him volunteering in the kitchen of the Gay and Lesbian youth center where I unwrapped prepackaged dinners for kids who dropped in after school. I'd come hoping for free counseling myself, but saw coming in the door I was too old by about three years and, realizing I was going to have to get used to doing without student health center psychiatric services, faced with BJ, hid my disappointment, feigning interest in volunteering. "Be careful," said BJ. "If you're not up on Barbara Streisand trivia these kid's'll eat you alive."

The kid to my left looked up from a magazine to ask: "Did Rudolf Valentino die of AIDS? He was gay, wasn't he?"

"That guy in sequins? Definitely gay."

"That was Liberace."

"AIDS hasn't been around forever, you know," I said. But as soon as I said it I saw, as far as any of us was concerned, it pretty much had.

I kept quiet. Things ran themselves. The center was evidently set up to provide three things: free meals, dissuasion against heroin use, and basketball. It defaultedly provided an enculturation course on icons a rapidly disappearing older generation had given pop gay status. I could put food in a microwave, I could play basketball, and I had Fridays off—all strong points for a volunteer. I didn't know Betty Davis from my ass. BJ and I met once a week to make out food orders at the kitchen table.

I'd been slack in going, so when BJ called a couple of weeks later, I assumed it was to make my slots more regularly-scheduled. But I got off the phone with the distinct impression that he'd forgotten I'd ever been a volunteer at all. He asked if I was coming to the next basketball game. They were going to have uniforms and what size was I? And did I want to drive to the beach with him that weekend?

So I packed some things in a bag—shorts, a shirt and decent underwear (in case I had a last-minute revelation BJ was the man of my life) and a microdot (the trip wouldn't be a complete loss even if it went badly). It was sunny. He pulled up. I ran out, swung open the car door, and jumped in.

He was following a baseball game. A scratchy voice recounted men hitting and running as we drove through ancient wet forests. The voice rose and fell with excitement. BJ constantly readjusted the volume. I can't follow a baseball game by radio, but he did for the time it took us to get into the mountains and the reception went out. The mountains were sudden. Fog whizzed past the sides of the car in thick wisps. I put the window down to take in a cold, wet breath of dark trees climbing one side of a peak, descending on the other. When a bank of fog went by, hitting me in the face with the force of a sprinkler system, I put down the visor mirror. My eyebrows were beaded with it.

"I brought a video camera," BJ said. "If you want to use it. When we get there. It's in the trunk."

Also in the trunk was a gallon jug of Carlo Rossi and a brown leather jacket. "Here," he said, handing it to me under the lights of the motel parking lot. I pulled it on. "Somebody left it. It's been there for months. I have no idea who it belongs to." BJ pulled out the jug. He got in the shower and I crashed on one side of the bed, feigning unrousable sleep.

Bright and early I went into the motel bathroom and downed the brown microdot with a glass of tap water. By breakfast things were starting to look beautiful in short, bursting glimpses, yet I was having a hard time judging what I could actually eat. I managed eggs Florentine before things got too blurry, then sat back, watching the yellow of egg run down the silver edge of my knife. BJ was saying something. He was mentioning how quiet I was. *Want to go horseback riding?* he was asking.

Sure, I said, having no idea what he was talking about. Something that would happen in the future, was all I could make out. Something he thought I would like. I was ready to like anything that didn't involve more food.

The clock at the waiters' station behind him was

nearing ten. The sun outside the window had glazed the sand between the restaurant and the beach. I hesitated a second as the waitress came, held my breath, feeling in my pocket for the lone twenty-dollar bill I'd brought—an extraordinarily small sum, considering all the things that could have gone wrong. BJ paid the bill.

The horses rented along the coast were small sandy animals, clustered in groups near tables and tents. Most of them were ponies. The families who rented them stood among them, fiddling with bridles and things at tables. At the first of these groups we walked up and the husband and wife both looked at us and shook their heads. "Nothing big enough for you guys," they said.

I would have just sat on the sand and watched the water, but BJ was into the horses. He had his heart set on riding. I ran ahead to the next group.

"Have you got a horse big enough for my friend?" I said.

They looked down the beach to where BJ was striding up. "Nope. Yer fella'd break a back of any of ours."

"These horses suck," I told BJ as he came up. "Let's try further along."

We walked together a little longer, and when we got near the next group I ran ahead again. "Got anything my friend can ride?" I asked. The husband looked at his wife. She squinted down the beach at BJ and shook her head. Further off stood the last group of horses on the shore. All ponies. I looked past the wife at the biggest of them. "Just half an hour," I said, handing her the twenty. BJ came up, pulling out his own wallet as she folded my bill away.

"Got some folks coming at noon," the husband said. His face tanned over at least fifty summers, his jaw still sharp. He bellowed a laugh toward BJ as he talked. "But if you want I can let you go out half an hour."

"Fine, fine," BJ said. The wife shook her head, looked at the horses, glanced at BJ, looked away. I put on my Walkman. Their daughter went out with us.

"Walk them!" the mother cried after us in a scolding voice. "Walk them!" after which I cranked up my Walkman as we took off. I'd ever been happier, U2 pouring into my ears, and let the horse run on the way back, pretending I'd lost control. Later that night in the motel's whirlpool I realized what BJ's video camera was for, and kind of stopped hanging out with him after that, although he did speak Spanish.

Boyfriend number two, an Italian, did not own a car. He read poetry in bed. Whenever I made a literary reference, he brought up Dante, which his accent made charming. He had published a hundred-page thesis in Italian on Aboriginal land rights, a copy of which he presented as a going away present when he moved to Australia three weeks later.

Boyfriend three was Gary Larsen's landscape architect. He owned a truck. Literary references he seemed not to register, either through confusion or disinterest, preferring vaguely racist comments. After camping, scuba diving or hiking, he would shower at my place, napping with abandon on the bed. I never asked if he'd studied a foreign language. He was earnest, and even seemed to have just run out of racist jokes when he decided to take a long vacation in Australia. He sent a post card months later, describing the inside of a shark cage.

I dated my barber, with neither a working car nor a second language, with whom I did not, perhaps with reason and perhaps without, attempt literary references before he moved to New Mexico.

From there I dated, in order: a tall Bostonian kleptomaniac (with whose aid I semi-unwittingly refurbished my wardrobe); a pale boy from the Channel Islands who claimed to speak French; a boy who spoke exchange student German haltingly, drove, and made several attempts at literary references himself, but who lived with his parents in Spokane.

Over a long and intermittent month, I dated Melanie from the harbor tours. One evening, as the brewery terraces cleared out in Belltown, she was sitting across from me, very straight in one of those old drugstore wire-backed chairs shaped like a Valentine's heart, in the garden court of Café Septième. A motorcycle leaned against the wall, half hid in the ivy, and I was wondering why I didn't move to Belltown, where there were interesting drunks and pool halls, and a vegetable plot with locally-made garden sculpture. Melanie sighed, fingering her gold-rimmed saucer with a white finger. She was saying: "It used to be enough just to wear a black T-shirt and jeans. Then I went back to Montana. Now it's all New Yorkers and complicated shoes. God." She yawned politely as we got up to leave. I walked her to a club. She gave me a kiss at the door and told me to call around three the next day.

Quick 'N Easy Recipe #7
Chocolate

Get a job at a coffee shop where they have chocolate.

Take lots of chocolate bars (don't worry, they don't really care) to your normal day job and eat like, three in a row. You'd forgotten chocolate contains caffeine, hadn't you? Well, now you can remember. Remember when you were a kid and you ate a whole chocolate bar and you really liked it? You were small and the chocolate bar was really big and it was better than swing sets. Now you're big and it takes three bars. When was the last time you ate three chocolate bars (dark Swiss) at once?

You're going to have childhood flashbacks you can enjoy for hours. Stand up and walk around and talk to your co-workers. You'll seem brilliant

and full of energy while they are dull and slug-
gish.

Type.

Spin in your swivel chair.

Pontificate at your boss.

Brush your teeth in the office bathroom.

Quick 'N Easy Recipe #8
Water

Water is cool. If you don't drink 8 glasses a day,
you're not living up to your energy potential.
Like a little sponge that's all dried up. You are
going to fill your body up with carcinogens and
die a horrible death (though medical science will
keep us breathing into our 90s, in most cases).

Find a water cooler. You can get almost all the
water you need from a water cooler at work.
Drink a lot. After a while, you'll realize you were
thirsty when you didn't even know it.

The best jobs have water coolers. At the end
of the day, you'll feel pretty good, and having
a reason to leave your desk every hour is
especially useful at boring jobs.

In the harbor tour's ticket booth, faces pushed maps and
fingers into the window all day, pointing and grumbling
in Japanese, shoving money for tickets. A boat deposited

tourists along the waterfront on the half hour. The booth's door opened with a sudden bang. Reflexively, I flicked my cigarette over the boardwalk, a clean shot into a planter of bougainvillea. It was Rob, of the lion-mane perm.

"The perfect cover, Ian, the perfect cover! Good thinking! Always one step ahead, you smart guy!" Rob winked.

It was his lunch hour.

My cigarette, I noticed, had resumed smoking in the planter.

Rob, gauging me, coquettish, reached into his pocket to produce a little pipe, the kind people make in junior high school shop class from curtain rod ends or cello tuning screws. Taking it from him, I admired it, giving it a perfunctory, appreciative sniff, smiling, handing it back. "I also brought these, just in case," he said, pulling out two sticks of incense, waving them frenetically with another grin. Customers came to the window. Rob sold them tickets, calming their worries, making several jokes at his own expense. Once they'd boarded the boat he muttered, "See ya, wouldn't wanna be ya" under his breath, a cleansing phrase he intoned after any cus-tomer contact. No one heard it. Most of the tourists were over seventy and somewhat deaf, if they spoke English. Rob pocketed the cash. Turning to me, repro-duced the pipe.

"Now?" I said. "Where the hell are we going to smoke

that thing? I'm not taking that into the bathroom at the mall."

"Right here, buddy. Hunch down under the counter. I'll keep a lookout for customers."

"You've got to be kidding."

"Go on, dude," Rob said.

The booth had windows on all four sides. The wharf was packed with tourists and the lunch crowd. A Klezmer set up to play. Two blue-haired ladies stood browsing through our brochure rack, mumbling to each other in German. "Hey!" Rob bellowed at them. "Got a great boat tour here today—right this way!" The women, frightened, turned away. Pressing the pipe into my palm, his hand on my head, Rob pushed me under the counter. It was awfully good pot.

It was hot under the counter. The floor beneath the carpet was metal, the heat from the sun beating on the boardwalk emanating up into the underside of the booth. I handed Rob the pipe. His hand came flapping down. Someone else had come up to the booth's window. After an amount of time I heard Rob call down "Are ya having fun down there, Ian?" I gave Rob my elbow. He pulled me up. "Well," he said, squinting into the pipe. "Looks like you're a fast little smoker!"

Rob, I said, blankly.

"You okay, buddy? You're not going to hurl, are you? You took down some major bud."

No, I answered, a sheepish smile.

"Okay, I'm going down! Cover me!" Rob shouted. Eventually, from under the counter, his voice rose up again. His face came up from the floor, with a smile half-grimace, the way his teeth were.

Rob . . . I said as he rose.

"I hate the fucking Q-tips the worst," Rob sighed.

Q-tips?

"The seniors—white hair on top and tennis shoes at the bottom. The captain taught me that one. What are you doing tonight? Want to help me move?"

Rob had lost his job as a trained nurse before becoming a harbor tour guide, and had to move.

Sure. Rob.

"You don't have to. If you don't want to. I'm packed already. I was really attached to this place—I got a nice view of the valley."

That's cool. Rob.

"Yeah, it is cool. You know what? I liked living alone. Not dealing with other people—not that I don't like people. But I like being by myself, too. And you know what? That's important. I'd stay there if I could, I really would. But that's okay."

That's cool. Rob.

"You totally don't have to if you don't want to."

Cool. That's cool. I'd like to help you. Rob.

"Meet me at the Crab Pot at five."

I sat in the ticket booth reading.

A woman with a scarf and sunglasses came to the window. She asked, "Do you remember when that place over there was run by Pakistanis and they had those two big rugs on the wall?"

"No, I said. "When was that?"

"About a year ago."

Her movements were sure but too sudden, her smile too wide.

"Oh, no, I just got out here this year."

"Oh, really, from where?"

"From college."

"You just got out of *prison*?"

"No," I said, looking to see if anyone had heard. "From college."

"Same thing." She smiled. "In what?"

"In college."

"No, silly." She looked at me. "What in college?"

"Oh. English, Art History."

"Mmm." She looked me over, moving closer. "College. Prison. I was there seven years. But I shouldn't say that. One of my husbands put me in a treatment place—4000 dollars a month, that kind of place. That was a real prison. You don't know what prison is. But you must read a lot. Did they teach you how to scan a paragraph?"

"I guess."

"You ought to go to that school up the hill. They teach

speed reading. I tried a class there. How long does it take you to read a paragraph?"

"I don't know. I read around three hundred pages a day, when I'm reading."

"What's your secret?"

"Good books?"

"Smart kid."

"Want to take a tour?"

"I wouldn't mind."

"One ticket?"

"Oh, so you're giving out tickets?"

"Well, selling them."

"Well. Bye." She waved. "Have fun. With the tickets."

"See you," I said.

"Don't ever start drinking and writing," she said, tottering down the waterfront. "All the greats did it. Don't ever do it. And don't marry for money."

"Yeah, okay, lady," I answered under my breath.

The waterfront was half a dozen garishly painted piers-cum-shopping malls, a backdrop of snow-covered peaks across the water. Standing at its edge, you felt you were in a timber town, if someone had gotten the colors wrong, fried a ton of vegetable tempura and salmon burgers, and raised a highway overpass. Rob was at the bar of the Crab Pot, talking to the bartender. He turned when he saw me. For a second I thought he might fall over. "You ready to go, buddy?"

"Hey." I sat beside him.

"Buy you a drink, Ian?"

"That's okay."

"Cigarette machine is broken," he said, motioning at it with his chin. I pulled a cigarette out. "You're supposed to quit," Rob said. "I saw you smoking today huh? Huh? This stuff's bad for you, Ian. Bad stuff. And what are you doing in a bar?"

"Looking for you."

"Yeah, hey, hey, but look. I got you a key chain." He pulled it across the bar to me, a miniature floatation device with "Crab Pot" printed on it.

"Cool," I said, swiveling my stool to look over the restaurant. A table of Koreans sat on a wooden bench eating crab cakes with plastic forks.

"Is it time to take off?"

"Yeah, yeah, let's blow this place." He said goodbyes to the bartender. "I always like to tip big," he said. "Those people work hard just like we do." He laughed, looking at me sidewise. "It's not easy dealing with these people all day. I can't go on yelling at them. That's why I needed a drink, Ian."

At the top of Queen Anne we stopped at the QFC. Rob didn't buy food I would normally eat. It was all white bread and colored cereals, lime green fizzy soda and flower-scented cat litter. His apartment was nice—two bedrooms hung over the valley, a freight train line running below, the hill green with vines, the sidewalk below pitted with chamomile. A second-hand breeze blew whiffs of chlorine and basil across the roofs of Magnolia's mansions. Rob wasn't quite packed—he was nowhere near being packed.

His rooms had the no-nonsenseness of a recent divorcée's apartment. An engagement ring in the soap dish by the kitchen sink, the butt of a Virginia Slims stubbed into a crack in the stairs. There were cat toys everywhere—curious plastic things you wouldn't think a normal cat would show an interest in. Rob's cat took an immediate dislike to me, her disposition only worsening when she found me looking under the bed. There was nothing there but a fresh copy of *GQ*.

Craning my head over a spider plant balanced on my lap, we pulled across the Ballard bridge. "You know, Ian, my new roommate has an enormous dick," Rob was saying from the other side of the plant.

"You've seen it?"

"I have indeed seen it. He pulled it out and laid it on the bar where we were drinking a few months ago." He turned to me.

"That's . . . weird, Rob."

"Yeah, can you believe that? He just laid it down on the bar." He went on. "Well, it was a private party. Maybe I didn't set the context up for you right."

We were quiet for a while. It was dark. I was thinking

I didn't want Rob hitting on me, mostly because I didn't want that to be the pick-up line.

An impromptu housewarming cookout was arranged on the front porch of Rob's new house. I served lime green soda into cups of ice. Rob's roommate was a retired Philadelphian fireman. The fireman's boyfriend, a younger, blonder version of the fireman, moved along the porch, orbiting around the fireman, perhaps in a state of anxiety that he might choose at any moment to lay his penis out on the porch rail for comments from guests. The yard overlooked a used car lot.

Rob paced the kitchen with the maniacal energy of a small dog in a house of strangers, men mumbling curses at him as they moved past. He shouted back at them, "Yeah, yeah, don't think I didn't hear that, Joe—just don't drop that coffee table—put it down! Yeah, right there where you're about to drop it." Across blue shag carpet, three men in leather vests lifted an armoire. Another stood in a corner adjusting a lampshade. A phone on a table rang. I picked it up. "Here, give it here," Rob said from behind an armoire. I handed it to him and he disappeared into the bathroom, closing the door. The room already held a clan of spider plants of astonishing proportions.

Someone gave me a cup of whiskey and I moved to the porch to sit on the stairs. A man in the yard threw lawn darts at a metal ring in the grass. "This thing's too small," he shouted at the porch. "Don't you have a bigger target?"

The fireman leaned over the rail. "Let me go upstairs and get my cock ring," he yelled.

Shoes clonked on the wood behind me. "Should I take you home?" It was Rob.

"Okay."

"Didja have a good time, Ian?" he said in the car.

"Sure. Everybody seemed pretty nice."

He looked over at me, trying to pick out sarcasm in my voice. It was dark in the car. There was a pause. "Sometimes you just have to take what you're given and roll with the punches, Ian. You know, we don't always like what happens to us. But you know what? Sometimes you just have to make the best of a situation."

"It's not a bad place."

"You got an eyeful of the car lot next door?"

"The parking lot lights are a little harsh. But you've got blinds." Pulling in front of my building, Rob saw for himself I was in a housing situation which made it unwise for me to crack on his. The scrubby bushes in the front garden had grown up to hide the side of the sad building. The rest rose over the bushes like a sad white scar. Tom Waits ground out of the second floor windows. By the steps, failed flowers sprouted, shoots of weedy-looking herbs Isaac had planted. He'd still been coming by a few weeks earlier to cull their tops or pull them up to trim their roots. The thought crossed my mind that he might have accidentally poisoned himself. There were empty beer bottles at the bottom of the stairs. Climbing up, I imagined I could hear Rob's voice inside the dark car's interior saying, "See ya, wouldn't want to be ya."

Lisa sprawled across a mattress eating grapes from a bowl, listening to the radio. She was halfway through a novel. Three more—all of equally daunting thicknesses—lay stacked neatly on the floor before her, her weekly reading material from the used bookstore.

"Hi," she said, finishing a paragraph. I sat down in a chair by the door. She rolled over, sighed, smiled and stretched, letting the book fall to the floor.

"My god," I said, slumping into my chair. She blinked. "I just had the most horrible evening."

"I'm sorry. What happened?"

"Want to go get drunk?"

"Well . . ."

"Come on."

"Okay." She smiled a big sleepy smile. "Let me pull some clothes on." She disappeared into the closet, came out in her underwear, but with sandals on, clomping around the room, poking under cushions and yawning. "Hmmm. Where did you want to go?"

"Somewhere with alcohol."

"Let me put some lipstick on."

"Someone called," she called from the bathroom. She was in a black dress flossing her teeth vigorously three inches from the mirror. In the refrigerator I found a banana, two cartons of Rice Dream, a peach, a bag of carrots, some lettuce.

"What did they say?"

"Not a lot. I told them you were out with a friend from work."

"Or something like that," I said.

"Or something like that," she said.

On Broadway, kids on heroin, or pretending or hoping to be, slumped on the sidewalk outside a cafe smoking cigarettes under the yellow light. We settled on a bar we knew. A group of Korean businessmen had collapsed across a table in the corner, one occasionally raising his head, looking around, perhaps checking to see if there wasn't any karaoke going on in some remote corner they had overlooked. None of them, as they lay with their heads in their hands, had taken off their glasses.

"I think I found a new boyfriend," Lisa said, sipping her drink.

"That's cool," I said. "That seems important."

"It's so cool."

"What's he like?"

"I don't know. He has a motorcycle. He wants to go to ¡Tchkung! next weekend. They're playing an outdoor concert in Oregon."

"You'd like it. Very green."

"I really want to ride on the back of a motorcycle to Oregon."

"Me, too," I said.

"What was so horrible about your day?"

"You'd have to meet Rob. Or not."

"You should hang out with people your own age."

"There aren't any."

"This whole city is your age. There's no one over thirty within a mile of Capitol Hill."

We looked reflexively at the Korean businessmen.

"Where did you meet Motorcycle guy?"

"Coffee shop."

"He's not on heroin?"

"I don't think the people in*side* the coffee shop are on heroin," she said. "Maybe the ones sitting in front of it. The people inside are pretty normal." She could get sentimental, then defensive—or defensive, then sentimental, about coffee shops. "I did have a weird experience there yesterday, though."

"Yes?"

"I looked up from my book . . . "

"Oy Jesus."

"Yes, Mr. Smarty Mouth. I looked up from what I was reading for a minute. The cafe was packed—the whole scene can change. In twenty minutes when you look up it's like you're in a completely different cafe. You know. I looked up and realized every single person there was wearing black. And I looked down and saw I was, too."

"The world is kind of fucked up," I ventured.

"That so goes without saying. But it was kind enough to give us Motorcycle guy. And Oregon."

We finished our beers.

"Should we pick up some more beer and head back to our own little scene of depravity?"

"Definitely."

I poked through the dozen rows of microbrews at the 7-11 on Broadway, losing the change to pan handlers, and we got back to the apartment nearly by twelve. Lisa opened a beer, setting it down on the floor and falling asleep. I stayed up, drinking hers, trying to get to a point in my mind where life made sense, even if only in a small way. Eventually I crashed, curled up in the bed, my chest to her back, an arm under her neck in the way experience eventually teaches you keeps it from falling asleep.

Quick 'N Easy Recipe #9 Late Night Snack

This tray of feisty hors d'ouevres makes a perfect late supper for two.

1 large tub of Crisco

Pepper

3 sticks of margarine

½ cup corn oil

½ pound uncooked hamburger

green olives

Ritz crackers

Glitter

Stuff the olives with a mixture of Crisco and margarine.

Douse with corn oil.

Pepper remaining Crisco, mix well with hamburger, sprinkle with glitter, and serve on crackers.

A mixture of 1 part grape juice, 1 part corn syrup provides a perfect complement to this meal.

Quick 'N Easy Recipe #10
Penny Bubble Gum Ice Cream

100 pennies

milk

Insert pennies into a gum ball machine. Remove gum, take home. Place in a bowl. Pour the milk over them.

Place bowl in freezer until frozen.

Melted remains can be poured over breakfast cereal.

Dating

In bars I got in the habit of letting men buy me a drink if they wanted to, playing shy till they saddled up closer. Then I started talking. About politics, or music, or books, and just kept talking, until most of them gave up, called it a day, said it was nice meeting me. We'd run into each other another couple of times in the same night. They'd smile and I'd grin back real big and if they were drunk enough they'd come back for more, but most of them didn't get that drunk. I bored their pants off. No—I kept their pants on by boring them. After a few beers like that retiring to play pinball, if they offer me another beer, I'd step outside, explaining I'd rather have a cigarette.

At twenty-three, I still had a perverse, yearning belief in fate which was more often than not confirmed. One night as I sat alone in my room fiddling with the instructions for an IKEA bed, I became convinced it was absolutely necessary to go out around midnight, and to a bar I detested. I tossed through a couple of tourist brochures, compulsively got dressed, went out on my bike, passed this bar twice thinking *no*, then pedaled back to it with a kind of hypnotic reserve and went inside.

There were three bars along the strip leading down

Pike Street toward downtown. One was for hipsters in black velour shirts with minor drug problems, one was for rave kids, and the last was for boys with baseball caps who played pool and darts, the kind of boys who simultaneously attracted yuppies and provided inspiration for their casual wear choices. The door to a bar halfway up the hill was propped open with a barstool. From the sidewalk, you could hear the jingling of a pinball machine inside.

The music was awful and energetic. People from the harbor boat were playing darts in a corner. I hung out with them until I'd been sufficiently snubbed to have an excuse to sit by myself at the bar, then found myself alone racking up pinball shots. Someone laid a beer on the glass of the machine, and as the last ball went past the flippers, I remembered a line from a poem, trying to catch it in my memory. It came back, familiar again, not a poem, but a dream I'd been having lately. I shivered thinking I could dream something often enough to know it by heart, but be completely unaware of it while awake. Off-work baristas, waiters and personal trainers leaned over the pool tables. Yuppies gathered in the corners, dressed like the baristas and waiters but more self-assured, shirts a little better-pressed and faces a little more tired close-up (but it was dark) watching and throwing darts. In one group stood one I'd seen before while delivering packages downtown—a man named

Mark with sad brown eyes and, as his story unraveled, a measured fluency in Japanese, an '88 Nissan, and an undergraduate degree in linguistics. After fifteen minutes I evidently hadn't bored him.

"You were in my office delivering packages," he said. "I'd just finished a job interview, and the interviewee brought the package to me. Are you still a bike courier?"

"No more," I said. "Did he get the job?"

"Actually, no. But he has a fine job already."

After another beer he was charming, with a square-jawed honesty ranging between smugness and self-deprecation. The bar closed. We stood outside. He was currently shopping for oriental carpets. His apartment had acres and acres of hardwood floors, he said, and his feet got cold at night, walking through the rooms. I decided I could not lay my head down that night until I'd seen acres and acres of hardwood floors. Acres and acres of hardwood floors seemed what I had been missing most for the past twelve months. I began losing my buzz. It was three in the morning, and he was still talking. "I wonder if you would come home with me," he said.

I looked at my bike on its rack, the bits of gum in the sidewalk. "I'd probably go home with you if you invited me," I said.

"All right. You're invited. Would you like to probably come home with me?" he asked, seeming grateful not to have to continue his monologue further.

Some leaves had fallen early along the sidewalk, their yellow edges glazed in the streetlight. I unlocked my bike, pushing it alongside us as we walked, my hand on its seat. He was talking again, his voice by turns soothing and nervous as it rose and fell—the tone one uses to call home a lost pet. "It's only eight blocks," he said. I think he half believed I'd take off on my bike at the last minute and disappear up the wet hill if the walk were too long.

A 1920s period apartment block sprawled like three Tudor mansions across blue squares of boxwood, fern, and ivy, slate walks and discreet niches for mailboxes, a mansard roof with gables, greening copper gutters and weather vanes. The people inside, you could see through their window panes, collected things like pewter and Delftware and copper aspic molds, and probably knew where to go to get an umbrella repaired. I put my head on this chest in his bed, ignoring two subtle attempts at seduction, then sensing something might depend on responding to the third. "I'm not that great at making love," I said.

In the morning we drove to Montlake for breakfast, splitting the bill. Then for several weeks we ate a lot of Thai food and sat by the roses behind his building, looking at the bay and the Space Needle. Then for a week I could tell he waited for me to call, debating calling himself. He dropped by on his way home from work trying to seem casual. I pulled him into my room, where the IKEA bed still lay in pieces by a sleeping bag on the floor. He stripped off his suit jacket and pants to help me figure out how put it together.

Quick 'N Easy Recipe #11
Candy

Candy is great. After years of only light to moderate sugar consumption, refined sugar can do amazing things to your system. Belgians are the world's largest per capita consumers of candy. Granted, they got ripped apart in two world wars, and in the 19th century they took over central Africa and were given to cutting people's hands off if they refused to work for them. But still, sugar can be a great thing.

Here's what to do:

Get a weekend job at a coffee shop where they sell expensive French candy and eat as much as you can. They have these great bonbons that are hard candy, pleasant in the mouth at first, then dissolving to develop spines that prick your tongue. Eat a lot of them. People who eat candy are the happiest people in the world.

Brush your teeth a lot.

Oh my, it's time to go home.

How time flies when one eats lots of candy.

Before meeting Mark, I'd never known anyone who counted out exact change for cashiers. As far as I'd ever known, you spent your bills until they ran out, and spent your change at the end of the month. Counting out exact change to get rid of it meant you didn't need change at the end of the month. Which suggested you probably never ran out of bills.

A plant store down the street from his building had put up a banner for a lawn and garden sale. "Can we get a lawn and garden?" I asked.

"Where on earth would we *put* it?" he asked.

I asked him why he still wanted to go to bars now that we'd met. "Should relationships be open?" I asked.

"Relationships should be open in principle," he said, "But for the moment, let's be monogamous."

When you take a lover and see his body naked for the first time, there are things you are bound to find not as you expected. Things you will know and eventually love more than the parts that didn't surprise you. Things that you recognize the first time, unfamiliar as they are. In his bathroom, scrubbed by housecleaners I let in twice a week after he left for work, I discovered that.

Weekends, his friends were all still there at the bar where we had met and he had always gone, but I didn't go much with him for fear of somehow jinxing things. When I did, the bar was the same, the ground floor scattered with lottery tickets, stairs leading past a neon-lit fish tank and up to a dark room hung with sports pennants and beer advertisements.

"Brandon, shouldn't you be home sleeping?" Mark was saying from the top of the stairs one night when I joined him.

"Oh my god," came a voice in front of him. On the landing, Brandon, in a half-open Oxford shirt, was coming down with two beers. "I have Sunday off," Brandon said, putting one beer up to his mouth, tilting his head in a way that seemed more to mime haughtiness than to aid drinking, spilling a little down the sides of his cheeks, arching an eyebrow at me. "Greg's downstairs playing darts," he said.

"Well, let's go find Gregory then," Mark said, following him. "Ian, do you need a drink? Yes, you need something to do with your hands before you start smoking." We walked to the other side of the bar. Two men gave querying glances at Brandon and me, moved to intercept us, faded away.

"This is my boyfriend Ian," Mark was saying, to men in suits, T-shirts, shorts. It turned out they were all lawyers, and all played darts together. After a round of handshakes, all devolved into lawspeak. Following Brandon to the bar, I noticed one of the lawyers looking straight into my face, and found myself unable to look away. His were the eyes I'd shared an earthquake with once in Café Paradiso.

"That's Trenton. Ian, Trenton. Trenton—my boyfriend Ian," Mark said.

"We've met."

In the cafe —I started to say—to Trenton—but Mark's voice hastened on with excitement and beer. I lost it in the noise of a crowd moving up the stairs toward the bar.

Brandon was dating one of the lawyers, but had a round-about way of talking that left it difficult to be sure which one. I asked if he knew all the guys playing darts. "That one," he said, nodding, "Blue shorts, geeky, smart, drops the darts a lot. That one, quiet, intense, graying. Your buddy there. Sane, and useful to know." He winked. "And that one, the one playing—" He motioned toward the guy from Café Paradiso. "Mad, bad. Dangerous to know."

Finding Lisa at home was increasingly rare. She'd sublet her room, following a startup to California.

Quick 'N Easy Recipe #12
Pork 'n Bean Soufflé Briquette aux Herbes Fines

10 small potatoes

1 can Pork 'n Beans

1 can cream of mushroom soup

1 cup croutons

1 egg white

anise

dill

tarragon

parsley

Slice potatoes thin. Mix well with other ingredients. Pour into a soufflé dish over croutons. Paint surface with egg white.

Fire in a kiln for 2 hours at 1200 degrees.

This dish makes an excellent conversation piece. I make one for my coffee table each Easter, breaking it up with an ice pick at the end of the year.

With rare exceptions, an afternoon of happy memories you and your loved ones will savor for years to come. But never forget, an unsupervised 3-year-old with an ice pick can easily scar an unsuspecting and beloved family pet for life in the time it takes you to turn around, and no amount of tears or prayers can bring back a punctured eardrum, or reverse an accidental partial lobotomy.

J. M. Parker

Quick 'N Easy Recipe #13
Red Pepper Sandwiches

(Had a better subject line for this post, but it's
an interoffice email system, and I didn't think I'd
push my luck too hard. It's cushy here — it's
8:00 and all I've done is email you.)

Capers

garlic

20 oz. can of pear tomatoes

Oil-cured Kalamata olives

good bread

raw spinach, basil

red pepper

Wine

cheese

Basil-flavored olive oil

raspberry vinegar

pepper

dried marjoram, rosemary, thyme

bowl

The perfect all-night eating experience, when
you feel like hanging out in the kitchen reading a
New Yorker someone left on the counter.

Requires stool (the kind you sit on).

Or a chair with lots of pillows, dragged into the kitchen.

Chop up garlic. Fry it in oil with red chili pepper flakes. Not much oil, as little as you can get away with. Before it browns, pour in tomatoes.

Simmer 10–40 minutes, breaking tomato chunks with spatula (bottom drawer).

Toast bread, drink wine, mix the oil and vinegar in bowl.

Dip bread in oil, with little spots of vinegar on the surface.

Really fucking yummy.

(Back next weekend.)

A banker, in retrospect, might have been a wiser choice. A dentist, a doctor, a rafting instructor or an underwater photographer specializing in shark cages might have been better choices. But lawyers were something I knew. My father had gone through several himself, on his own slow rises and descents. Smiling, friendly, capable of mental acrobatics my own conscience couldn't quite extend toward, lawyers took up more space than ordinary men. White fingers splayed to exhibit various earnest gestures, they whispered things making quiet rooms jump, then sauntered into elevators redolent of aftershave, descending to bars to drink glasses of Merlot like medicine, the wool of their suits stretching slightly at their joints.

At Mark's we played UpWords on the carpet, drinking wine and talking about what we wanted more than anything else in the world. He wanted to be happy and in love. I wanted a million dollars, and to take a ferry to Alaska, a boat to Uelen, and the TransSiberian railway to Finland. He said if I had a million dollars I could afford to take a plane. My job was ending in a few months, but I was be glad to do something different for the winter, but would miss having extra money, and expected to live simply for the next months. He wanted to keep doing things with me even if I was going to be poor, and hoped I wouldn't mind if he paid for concerts and stuff because he'd hate to think he was breaking me whenever he wanted to do something. How much he made every year was a pretty huge amount of money, but it was less than that, really, he said, since he had student loans, and I said if he was making that much I wouldn't feel too badly about it.

We sat on the bench behind his building looking at the city and the Space Needle, talking about how I wanted to see the world and he said that as he talked about how he felt about life, he felt it more sincerely than he ever had before, which was a good thing, he said. He wanted to talk about dreams. He never remembered his dreams. If I slept with him, he thought maybe my dreams would rub off on him. I was curious what he dreamed about as he turned in bed beside me. When I woke up in the mornings, as he came in from the shower to kiss me, I had the odd sensation he was taking my dreams away. I forgot them as he woke me and couldn't concentrate on what they had been.

I told all this to Lisa when I got home. She'd gotten accepted to UW. Unsure about loans she'd need, she wanted to meet Mark, so the three of us went to Re-bar with a couple of Mark's friends, Greg, a tall lawyer from another firm, and a couple of other guys from Greg's firm. Lisa and Mark pressed close together on the sidewalk in front of us, deep in conversation, but once inside, Lisa, the music rising, turned to me, asking for help to lift her up onto a speaker, to dance above the crowd. "Watch out for my shoes," she called, as I lifted her upward, "Not for the shoes, for your hands," then set off doing an extemporized Charleston on top of the speaker.

As the crowd filled the club, Mark and I left the four of them still carousing at the door. In the silent street outside, he said, "She's fantastic."

Isaac came back from Oregon toward the end of the summer and called for a conversation that, in the end, degenerated into his saying, "Sometimes I just miss you. I missed you a lot this summer. Do you ever miss me?"

"No."

"Not even a little?"

"Nope."

"Well. Sometimes I think about you."

"Well. Sucks to be you."

A pause. "Is that how you're going to be?"

"I guess so."

"I guess I'd better go then."

"Bye."

Quick 'N Easy Recipe #14
Love Potion #9

Bottle of dark zinfandel

beer bong

whipped cream

Pour the wine into the top of the bong, wait until excess air goes to top. Take a deep breath. Insert bottom of bong into mouth. Lift top of bong above head.

For special occasions, spread whipped cream over the top before use.

Or just take a hit off the whipped cream canister.

There were benefits that fall. Politicians were giving dinners. I had an ill-fitting tuxedo left over from a semester in the university chorale, so Mark took me along. Receiving lines and speeches, a friendly governor with a lopsided, disarming smile, lesbians, awkward and proud in glittering dresses and strangely piled hair. At the end of them people rose to dance to strangely optimistic 1960s music, dances appearing to have actual steps.

Mornings, Mark asked me to stay in to open the door for the cleaning lady. After a few months, he didn't see why I was keeping my own place.

"What do you want?" I'd ask him.

"I want to fall in love," Mark would say, and nights, at his place, as I turned in my sleep, his arms followed me.

Lisa left more recipes taped to the refrigerator:

Quick 'N Easy Recipe #15
Bongwater Soufflé

Bongwater

2 boxes Kraft macaroni 'n Cheeze

¼ cup raisins

¼ cup granola

Maraschino cherries

1 tube Chap-stick

Def Leppard album

Boil until thickened, cook as a soufflé, or serve on crackers.

Quick 'N Easy Recipe #16
Kitchen au Flambé

Make chicken soup with fresh chicken and lots of bay leaves and fresh basil. Don't clean up afterward. Leave stray bay leaves, dried rice and basil on the stovetop. Then make Quick 'n Easy recipe #2, spreading piles of capellini pasta across the stovetop. Wait a week. Ignore the stray bay leaves and dried pasta. Light up the stove (Quick 'n Easy chefs know gas works best).

Leave the room for at least 5 minutes.

When you return you'll have Quick 'n Easy Recipe #15: Kitchen au Flambé.

This recipe works best in kitchens with substandard electrical wiring, when housemates are out of town. If an ex is present, use him to help put out the flames (or call the fire department).

Drink some wine. Now that's Quick 'n Easy!

Exterminators arrived in our building at eight o'clock on a Saturday morning to bomb out the roaches. Grudgingly climbing from bed to leave them to it, I wandered two blocks to the park, trying to nap on a bench as joggers went by, the scrape of tennis shoes on gravel lulling me to sleep.

"What do you think?"

It was Lisa. She'd said whatever was going to happen to her hair would take three hours and cost a day and a half's wages. Eyes closed, I had a dozen easy compliments ready.

"It looks good. It suits you." I stretched on the bench.

"You are positively full of shit," she said. "Your eyes aren't even open. But I brought you coffee anyway."

"Seriously. I think I like it."

"I don't know." She nudged me over, sitting down. It was streaked blonde—not much lighter than before. "They said if I didn't like it I could go back and do more."

"It's perfect." The last time she'd spent three hours at Rudy's, it cost a day and a half's wages, and came back neon red. She handed me the coffee. One sip brought the leaves on the trees and the sky into focus. "But I thought the whole point of doing something different to your hair was so nobody can tell the difference."

"What kind of point is that?" she said. "That doesn't seem like much of a point to me."

"It's great."

"I hope you're right. It's for something kind of important."

"A job?"

"No. More of a boyfriend."

Brandon, I thought, but after a few more sips of coffee thought better of asking. "Motorcycle guy?"

"No, now it's horse guy. Actually, it's his parents. You're going to hate me. He asked me to move in."

Chugging the caffeine, my heart went to my gut. The joggers circled the track under the blue sky.

"He lives on a farm with his mom and dad," she was saying. "But it's not like that. His parents are Danish, and they have this whole village of tiled roofs out on an island, and he lives there. I'm going to go and help take care of the horses and work in the restaurant with him."

"So it's a haircut for the horses."

"More or less."

"You're happy."

"I think so. He has a car. We'll be back in the city whenever."

"What's he like?"

"He's not Brandon."

I stuck my tongue down into the cup to get out the sugar and foam at the bottom. "Anything else?"

"They grow arugula."

"Good things." I looked at the sky. A jogger passed.

"Don't freak on me, Ian. Don't freak on me. You look like you're going to freak."

"Don't flatter yourself."

"You think I'm selling out."

"'Selling out' doesn't mean anything to me."

"The hell it doesn't. Let's go somewhere."

"Anywhere. You choose."

"So get up. Before I have the urge to take up jogging, or you take up with a jogger."

I took her hand.

"More coffee? I have a successful haircut, it's a beautiful day, in two hours we can go home to sweep up dead roaches without serious risk to our health. It's not like you don't have half a dozen junior attorneys in your back pocket for a rainy day. You forgot the Italian who writes you poetry every week. I can forget about Brandon."

"You read my mail?"

"The postcards. Your write him back. Don't try and tell me you don't. You're cute, but nobody sends letters that thick to someone who doesn't write back."

We walked to the market, eating strawberries and drinking shots of espresso, but we didn't have a good time. Together, we made a pretty good argument that if a relationship is over, it's over. Then five minutes later, after coffee and a bagel, we couldn't think of a good reason *not* to keep sleeping with him. "I wish I could just grow up," she said. "Don't know how. Don't know what to do." She spent weekends away, either grooming horses or being groomed by her sort-of boyfriend for his parents, she didn't say which. She was leaving, and without expecting it, I felt myself exactly where I'd been six months before.

Quick 'N Easy Recipe #17
Classic Dinner Party for Four

What you will need:

Guests

Grill

Altoids

Bread

Wine

Remy Martin

5 lbs. Pacific Salmon

Onions

Peppers

Basil

Tomato

Lemon

Pasta

Cheese

Olive Oil

Garlic

Salt

Candles

Salad

Red Vinegar

Olive oil

Vodka

Diet Coke

Stash vodka inconspicuously in kitchen for later use.

Open the first bottle of wine. Drink.

Put a large pot of water on to boil for the pasta.

Lay the salmon out, cover with basil, onions, red pepper and tomato, in that order. Salt lightly.

Prepare the grill outside. Place salmon on grill.

Inside, wash peppers and place them in the oven at 375.

Dice 5-6 cloves garlic very fine.

Chop ¼ cup basil very fine.

Crumble ¼ cup blue cheese.

Place the above in three piles on the cutting board (for extra-pretentious guests, also dice ¼ cup oil-cured Kalamata olives).

Rinse lettuce and salad things.

Take the bottle of wine outside. Look in the grill.

Finish bottle. Put it in the trash outside. When your partner asks what happened to the bottle, laugh and tell him you used it to season something.

Chop the salad things. Scatter pine nuts over the salads, more or less depending on the pretentiousness of your guests. Mix a dressing of vinegar, olive oil. Pepper.

By the time you finish the dressing, you should be halfway through the second bottle of wine.

Fortunately, your guests will bring more wine. Unfortunately, they don't drink, and brought white wine which hasn't been chilled. But you can always use it the next time. Put it in the refrigerator and offer them some red.

Seat them.

Bring out the roasted peppers, cheese, and bread. Place the peppers on a mound of basil and serve with knives. Make your partner talk to them, listen and smile while you finish your glass of wine, then put the pasta in the boiling water on the stove, take a quick swig from the vodka, and run outside the check the fish. It will be done, but you can leave it on just another minute while you ruminate over vodka. Your partner will come out to say you're being rude.

Leave the fish on the grill. Return to the kitchen, stir pasta, put salads on the table, with dressing.

Change a CD. Glance at your partner. Discretely pour him more wine. In the kitchen, take another swig of vodka. Go back out to the grill. Put the salmon on a serving tray and take inside. Try not to spill or drop it. Slice the lemon into 6 pieces and place on a dish. Pour another glass of wine. Take fish and lemon to the table. Take advantage of the small air of semi-sobriety still lingering about you to say something charming before it's too late.

Drain pasta, divide into serving bowls. Fry garlic and oil, put crumbled cheese and basil over the pasta, and before garlic browns, pour evenly over the serving bowls.

Swig vodka.

Stuff mouth with Altoids.

Stir each plate so the cheese gets into the crevices of the pasta, and the oil mixes in (this way, the pasta doesn't stick together, but still stays hot). Bring to table.

Open another bottle of wine, pour yourself a glass. Keep the bottle close. Notice your guests are drinking diet Coke, and that their full wine glasses are sitting on a table across the room. Pour yourself another glass. Take a few bites of salad. Poke at your fish. Smile when they compliment you. Dig your fingers into the underside of your chair and fix your guests with an interested expression, keeping the room in focus. From time to time, follow the conversation to see that your partner is providing amusing anecdotes. When he fumbles, pour more wine.

Remain balanced in your seat.

A Death in the Family

When I stepped onto the boat Monday, I thought I was being fired. Lana, our supervisor, stared at the deck in contemplation, the tour guides circling round her, eyes lowered. Melanie glanced up, winking a smile.

"Good *morn*ing, Ian," Lana said, glancing at her watch. Melanie sighed, and everyone else harrumphed, standing back.

"We have good news and bad news today," Lana began. "The *good* news, I think you all know." Lana looked around at us. "The season is finishing up. You've all done a *great* job and we hope you'll come back next year. And I'm sure you've heard the bad news, Ian. We've all just shared a moment of silence." The war had been declared that morning while I lay sprawled on Mark's bed. Fallout was due in New York any minute. Mark was probably already in a car headed up the coast to Canada.

"Jerry Garcia died last night," Melanie whispered. All eyes in the cabin shone on me like gapers at a highway accident.

"Oh," I said. My response seemed briefer than expected. I amended it to, "Oh my."

Looking away with disappointment, they turned back

to Lana. "Well, try to keep up a good humor on the boat. Sometimes it helps to talk. I want to take a few minutes here in case anyone has something to share. Matt? Ian? Melanie? Rob? Did you have a memory you'd like to share?"

"Uh, no."

"Let's all join hands. I was at the memorial service last night, and it was really touching. People were really into remembering in a good way. I bought everyone these bracelets," she said, pulling a handful of laced hemp from her bag. "It's a sad day for everyone, but try to remember the good things about Jerry if you can, and not let it affect our work any more than necessary."

Matt fingered a bracelet. Lana's beeper started going off.

The days grew shorter. The tourists, their vapid energy, thinned out. "It's food stamp season," Melanie said that afternoon, a foot propped against the ticket counter, as a Japanese couple fingered a brochure. "Good anywhere, any time. Last year I was afraid I'd get weird looks at the Quick Mart when I got mine, but I've seen people buying prosciutto at Delaurenti with food stamps. Mark my words. A couple more weeks like this and the people at harbor tours central are going to call it quits for the year."

She frizzed her hair, letting it fall tangled over her face. We talked about the new story she hadn't worked on since she got flu. She was writing, weekends, at her sister's, next door to a boy's reform school, about an affair she re-started with a Russian alcoholic. I'd been sitting in my room for a week trying to write. "Real writers do that," she said approvingly, through a pair of pink sunglasses. Halfway through telling me about her ten-year marriage to a Houston lawyer with a gambling problem, we realized it was six and we should have left an hour ago. She snickered as I pulled a shirt over my boat tours uniform to go.

Rob drove me to Capitol Hill and we walked down Broadway together. He looked at everything twice. "In the '80s, Capitol Hill was all skinheads and one gay disco where guys got beat up all the time," he said. "Then in 1989 two skinheads came banging on some guy's door at two in the morning and the guy's boyfriend hit them over the head with a two-by-four. And now it's gay," he said. But he still didn't get why they needed so many cafes. We drove past the cathedral and the bridge and across the canal. Below the bridge Rob lit a joint, pointing through the fog across the water to where a long slab of yellow light burned between the boats. "You know that place?" he said.

"Ivar's," I said. "The upscale branch. Where Q-tips go if they can handle a taxi ride and want to eat fish in an authentic Northwestern setting, but without Indians."

"Right you are, buddy. Right you are. Two points in the harbor tours scorebook. Ever eaten there?"

"I've seen photos." I put down my window. "They have an authentic Tlingit canoe hanging from the ceiling, and Ivar's personal collection of fanciful traditional-style masks."

"But as far as the grub goes you know virtually zero."

"Expensive, I'd guess. The same fish they serve on the waterfront, but baked on a Native American-style open barbecue pit and served with an array of succulent award-winning sauces, with lemon-mascarpone gnocchi instead of French fries."

Rob tapped the steering wheel lazily. "How many times a day do you recommend it to people?"

"Less than the restaurant in the Space Needle. It's easier to give directions to the Space Needle."

"Grub, buddy, I'm talking grub," Rob said. I handed the joint back to him, with some reservations, as he jerked swiftly to turn around the lake. "You want to get something to eat?"

"We could go back to my place."

"Ivar's has a nice salmon steak."

"No doubt, but I was planning on paying my rent this month."

"And what would you think if I told you the harbor tours was paying for it?"

"Then I'd think you were full of shit."

"What if I just said it was my treat, then?"

He pulled into a parking space. Bushes glistened under garden lamps in the fog. Inside a dark little red room with couches and a cabinet of masks, Rob said, "Hiya. We'd like a table for two."

At the far side, a long table of Japanese men and women in elaborate dresses ate in silence. The lights across the lake winked in the fog.

"What have you got as far as a good salmon steak?" Rob was saying, ordering for both of us. "So what do ya think?" he asked. "Nice, huh? We ought to come down here for lunch every day."

"The canoe's bigger than I imagined," I said. Salmon steaks came to the table, laced with béchamel and mint, but the company closed the boat tours for the season two weeks later.

At Christmas I flew back to see my family, and figure out what was next.

INTERLUDE

Back at my parents' place, I found myself playing mental games I'd played as a child—or rather, games I'd played all my childhood so automatically and unconsciously that I'd never thought of them as games till now. Without conscious effort, I began counting the steps across the lawn to the front porch from walks with the dog. *Forty-eight, forty-nine, fifty . . .* The game was: a very special sort of nuclear bomb would drop on the neighborhood tonight. If you didn't make it back to the house within a hundred steps, you'd be frozen forever, right where you stood. Or not frozen. Plastified, as if carved in stone. It came from having nothing better to think about. *Fifty-seven, fifty-eight . . .* Hopefully, the dog wouldn't have to pee crossing the street. Otherwise, once frozen, we might be hit by a car. These games just came, and I played them, wishing I could shut off my mind. But I had. This was what happened when I did.

More unsettling was a game I'd played as a child of "who was watching." This game in particular resumed with alarming regularity: Someone was watching as my feet crunched along the lawn now—or now as I reached the house, and now, as I opened the door—or now, laying gloves on the hall table—vague expressions on unvisual-ized faces showed reactions ranging from surprise to envy. I'd learned to play the faces at will. My old girlfriend watched as I drove down the street to my parents' house because she'd be impressed by the lines of oaks and the fact that I was listening to NPR. I wanted to share what I was doing with someone, but had no one to share it with, and wasn't doing anything.

Again and again I annoyed myself, slipping into these habits when I wanted to be "writing." Driving across mountains and hills cut red from bulldozers, I thought I could write about that. With the window down and the car speeding across the asphalt, my watchers became fleeting now. Across the mountains toward West Virginia, there was fog and less bulldozers. There was no view through the fog. The only way you could tell you were in the mountains was that the road still angled up, and the air had a dampness you could taste, emanating a different scent higher up. Shacks and bungalows pushed against hillsides in the fog and brambles, with glimpses of richer, dark green spaces higher up. Rhododendrons with branches so thick you could climb in them, as a grown man. *It doesn't matter what you do in your mind*, I told myself. *You'll live an estimated eighty years on this planet, and it will matter very little whether you thought obsessive and bizarre things during that time.*

Restaurants crammed into roadside cabins, smoky

with generic cigarettes, full of the thin-fingered men who sat smoking them, redecorated sometime during the late sixties, windows oriented so that the view of the mountains behind was blocked, and out of them was only fog and a road leading down to a post office. There were only pink-skinned men, with yellow-tainted creases in their faces, from smoking and squinting. I ate two plates of barbeque, oily and full of MSG. No one was cheerful, though the waitress seemed to know everyone. I kept my eyes on my plate, my last glimpse of the place a greasy yellow smear of barbeque sauce left across its surface. It was a sticky, damp hot-cold day, yellow sun through the fog. I sweated in my coat in the parking lot, my nose and fingers cold. The radio said the haze was smoke from a forest fire to the north. Bulldozers sat on ledges along the road, making way for a highway through the mountain. Traffic, as the sun set between the hills, was rerouted up a straight sheet of black rock a thousand feet high, zigzagging back and forth every fifty yards.

The East is strange with its whites and its blacks, its Indians and its old and its young. The old sitting on porches in the evening and the young sitting on car hoods in parking lots in the evenings. Even if no one still alive had done anything to anyone, someone's ancestors had done something to someone's in ways meant to leave marks. Old and young, everyone went on living the best they could, and whites, too, went on living the best they could, as they always had, helping or hurting the others when they could, depending on their temperaments, their fellows' temperaments, and what they read in newspapers. Unable to control them as they once had, they would control things as much as they could. White children wouldn't always know what it was that made them fear the blacks, and black children wouldn't always know why they were sometimes angry, then sometimes shy. Eventually they might grow to know it. But no one was encouraged to think about these things, or to ask questions, and their children couldn't ever really see the same, since they lived in such different circumstances, having seen such different things, with no one to help them understand, and it was a dreary place with its history. Dreary if you talked about it, drearier if you didn't.

The smoke was a little clearer in the valley. Guys in overalls with no shirts and girls in velvet cloche hats with big sunflowers smoked, sitting in uncomfortable Shaker-style chairs. It was seventy-four degrees outside, and everyone was being ironic, but it didn't feel like Christmas.

Mail came from Lisa.

Quick 'N Easy Recipe #18
Holiday Pork 'N Bean Liver Loaf with Prozac

Another holiday treat to remind the faithful family of God's promises

3 cans of Pork n' Beans

1 package plain gelatin

1 cup water

Chicken livers, chopped fine

small ornamental doves

bag of red licorice (festive!)

Birthday candles

Ground Jamaican Allspice

1 tsp. Prozac, ground fine

Mix Pork 'n Beans, water, liver, gelatin and chill in a cross-shaped mold.

Decorate with ornamental doves and licorice.

Cover with birthday candles.

Sprinkle on Prozac and Allspice.

Quick 'N Easy Recipe #19
Very Veggie "Jesus Day" Jesus

Sometimes, with all the hustle and bustle of the holidays, we forget that Christmas Day is really Jesus Day. This holiday dish reminds us that Jesus is a vegetarian who walks on water and hates heretics. I like to serve it regularly, because, really, every day should be Jesus Day.

This dish is a meal in itself and more fun to watch than the Charlie Brown Christmas Special.

You will need:

37 packages of Veggie Burger mix

40 cans of Root Beer

10 green peppers, diced

10 onions, diced

1 large can of Crisco

Salt

2 pounds cherry tomatoes

2 nails for each member of your household (and a few extra in case they get bent)

1 large cross

17 clothes hangers, bent straight

20 cans Tuna in vegetable oil

Blue food coloring

Red food coloring

Colored Christmas Tree lights

1 Heretic

Gasoline

Bend the coat hanger wires into a Jesus shape (approximately 4 feet high—or larger if you like).

Mix the root beer, veggie burger mix, vegetables, salt and Crisco and mold the combination over the coat hanger wires into a Jesus shape while praying and meditating.

Bake at 350 for 1 hour.

Spread the tuna on a flat surface and color with blue food coloring. This will represent fish (get it?) and water that the Veggie Burger Jesus can walk on. Shape waves from the tuna with fork tines using Crisco as needed.

Set Jesus upright on the Tuna and support as needed.

Pour red food coloring over Jesus' head (this represents that he died—get it?). Drape the Very Veggie Jesus with the colored Christmas tree lights. Set the cross upright behind Him. Arrange tomatoes artfully in the tuna.

Have your housemates or others present drive the nails through their hands, ears, nostrils, cheeks, eyebrows, nipples, or other body parts (use ice to numb body parts first, and always clean afterward with peroxide or gin).

Tie the heretic up and burn him/her.

Note: For added effect, you can also burn the Very Veggie Jesus itself, and the cross. If you do this, though, you will need to make 2 — one for eating, and one for burning. Praise God.

Quick 'N Easy Recipe #20
Magic Cajun Pork 'N Bean Sauce

4 cans Pork 'n Beans

1 can Tuna

1 cup Tabasco sauce

2 tbsp. Black pepper

1 cup corn syrup

Drano, to taste

Open and drain the liquid from the Pork 'n Bean cans into a large bowl, discarding the solid beans. Do the same with can of Tuna. Mix well, adding Tabasco, corn syrup, Drano and pepper.

This sauce goes well with avocados, and also makes an excellent salad dressing and/or expectorant.

Lisa had left another recipe taped to the refrigerator.

Quick 'N Easy Recipe #21
MDMA Salad

Salad:

    1 carrot, peeled

Vinaigrette:

    2 capsules MDMA

    Water

Kurt's Dead

There were thirty-two dollars in the bank when I got back to Seattle. Two hundred dollars' worth of food stamps and a gift membership to Mark's gym had come in the mail. A message on our voicemail from the bike couriers asked me for a call back.

Lisa opened the door around five.

"Oh my god," she said. "Look out. The roaches are back. They're worse. Normally it's just the big old roaches that hang around. But it was warm while you were gone. It's like summer again. Big ones, little ones. I hate the little ones. At least the big ones have character. How was home?"

"Well, I'm back."

"That's been my general experience, also. Welcome back."

I sorted through the dishes in the sink and made some coffee. There was a roach in the coffee pot. I rinsed it down the sink. Lisa rolled a joint. I lit a cigarette.

"You're still smoking those things?" she said, picking up the pack from the counter and reading the label. "What the hell. Phillip Morris has a toll-free customer service number for people with health concerns. Like, what are you going to call them about? Where's the phone? I have to try this. Hello," she said after a minute. "Yes, I think I have lung cancer."

"They put me on hold," she said. In the bedroom, I was pulling on fresh clothes. "Got a date tonight, I take it?"

"In a couple of hours," I said.

"You're coy. Same lawyer? New one?"

"Same."

"Aces."

I shrugged.

"For his sake, I hope he has a dishwasher. The landlady promised to spray for roaches again. If you leave, too, it might actually start getting lonely around here."

"What happened to Horse guy and the Danish farm family?"

"Long story. Mind if we just went out for coffee? Not that this isn't good coffee. My treat. I just don't want to talk about Horse guy."

We walked around the corner to Café Roma. Standing in line to order, she kept her eye fixed on a window table. The guy in front of us, ordering two coffees, was trying to give one to the barista, who wasn't having it. "I never drink while I'm working," she said.

"What do you want?" Lisa said. "But do me a favor and go grab that table over there. I'm attached to that table. I never sit anywhere else. My chair's the one by the wall." She came back with my coffee and something for herself in a glass with whipped cream protruding from the rim.

"All I ordered was a latte," she said, sidling into her seat. "They're starting to get decadent here."

"That's not decadent," I said. "Decadent is checking into the Four Seasons, ordering the whole room service dessert menu, emptying the minibar, and shooting heroin in the whirlpool bath with porn stars while reading *The New Yorker*. Rome was decadent. Babylon was decadent. That—if my guess is correct—is a dandified mochachino in a Pyrex glass."

"I stand corrected."

"So how's office life?"

"Florescent lights, fake plants, Impressionist prints, classical music in the elevators. With something called casual attire. They're very insistent about it. If they wanted me to put on a uniform, I'd put on a uniform. But they never really put their finger on what it is. It gets expensive, these stupid clothes that aren't me, but are somehow supposed to have my personality. I sometimes buy ugly cheap clothes just to protest. And I feel awful wearing them. The bike couriers make it worthwhile. Though they may all be gay."

"I'll let you know next week."

"They called me down to human resources, so, being a human resource, I went. They asked if I wanted benefits, so I was like, *what kind of benefits?* I'm still looking at the booklet. They don't cover anything holistic. I may say no and save myself thirty dollars a month. I was always kind of a Christian Scientist anyway."

"Except for the Christian part."

"The rest of it, though. I always assumed death would be like, when you're a child and you think closing your eyes makes the world go away? Except it actually works."

We turned our chairs to watch the sunset over the drugstore across Broadway. "But we must talk," she said, grabbing my wrist. "Our home life is beginning to have a negative impact on my work environment. Yesterday, my boss came over to my desk. My backpack was behind her, and I was sitting there the whole time over a computer screen, hoping to god she wouldn't turn around to see the roach I was watching crawl out of my bag. I'm not completely clear on the nuances of office culture, but I'm thinking that would be bad."

"Could be."

"So you're off to the bike couriers?" Lisa said.

"For a while again."

"You'll be buff."

"I'll probably just get skinnier."

"That's what happened to Brandon. But the cool thing with him was, when you get that much exercise all day, your metabolism goes way way up, so he could get super toasted on just one beer. We saved a lot of money that way. Until he got his ulcer."

She sipped her coffee, gazing out the window. "You remember that time you came home and said some guy had told you the most honest thing you'd ever heard anyone say? Is it like that with that lawyer?"

Pulling my coffee to my lips, I didn't feel like swallowing, and put it back down.

"Forget it," she said. "You're smart enough to figure out what you want. I'm sure he's a nice guy."

"What's that supposed to mean?"

"Whatever the hell you think it does."

"We ought to get out of town and go hiking."

"Yeah."

"This weekend?"

"Sure. Or, well, some time."

It was raining. Nag Champa floated from the Indian store in Broadway Mall. On the sidewalk lay fewer sprawling drunks than at the height of summer. A bearded man stretched under the awning of the SeaFirst ATM. Lisa laid a nickel on his bare belly. Flinching in his sleep, he rolled over, letting the nickel roll along the sidewalk. The awning shuddered with a wind that wasn't unpleasant, and I was glad to be back in a place where you don't bother asking yourself if you feel at home.

"Kurt's dead!" Lisa shouted into a gust of wind at an intersection, but only a middle-aged man in a trench coat walking a dachshund on the other side of Broadway was there to hear her.

She spent weekends away. Her mail piled on her desk. Brandon postmarked a card from Hong Kong with a recipe for barbecue. Lisa left notes on Tupperware in the refrigerator:

Quick 'N Easy Recipe #22
Pineapple Shish-Kebabs with Magic Cajun Bongwater Pork 'n Bean Sauce

Chicken, cut into 1-inch chunks

3 green peppers

1 can pineapple chunks

Bongwater, with ash

Pork 'n Bean juice, drained from can

3 tsp. Root Beer

salt

"Why don't you move in with me?" Mark asked.

I said I'd give it some thought.

I Love You

What happened that weekend made up my mind.

We were supposed to go to a rave on a pier downtown, Lisa, Brandon and me, and Todd from the bike courier base. We dropped in a parking lot by the pier—unadvisedly, it turned out, as the Seattle fire department arrived five minutes later, closing the place down to check out an over-loaded sound system. We stood with the crowd, watching orange loading cranes shift containers at the far end of the bay, then moved to Pioneer Square to drink orange juice. A giant billboard reading "OK Cola" was the only stable thing outside the plate glass window, above the moving stream of traffic lights.

"We're finally being marketed to," Lisa said, eyeing the lit moonscape of the billboard.

"About damn time," Brandon said, leaning firmly into his juice. "My general sense of self-appreciation just shot up fifty points."

"I'm not any thirstier," said Todd.

For a minute the word "OK" rose among us, a symbol and summary of the whole evening, a prediction of the future, a comment on everything passing in the street outside below the billboard.

"Do you think they planned it that way for people who were tripping?" Todd asked. He'd ripped his pants climbing a fence when the firemen arrived. Brandon and I went into the cafe's bathroom with him to pin them up. Toilet paper all over the floor—some kids coming in before us had trashed the place.

Back at the parking lot, some people from the bike courier place said the rave wasn't going to happen. They'd convinced us to take them somewhere to chill out and wait to see if the party started back up again in the morning, since no one ever really got there until four or so anyway. They asked if Brandon was okay to drive and Brandon said he didn't think so, gazing at his car as if it were something new and terribly interesting to him (the edges of it, he said later, were quivering as if waiting to go). They looked at me. They all piled into the car and got quiet. I sat in front. I turned on some music.

"I can't believe they let people drive cars at all," I said.

"Well, they make it as painless as possible," Lisa said. "Just go. There are brightly-colored reflective markers telling you which way to go—see?—which lane to stay in, and—look there—even how fast to go." I felt like a jet-lagged Parkinson's victim on opioids. But the streets were straight, the lights changed colors when they wanted you to stop or slow or go. Todd pointed out a thirty-five mile per hour speed limit sign, and I was sure

I'd somehow driven in the night through time itself and aged a decade, the sign announcing it.

Shrubbery hummed in the wind, in the streetlights, vibrating at the car windows. I stopped at the top of Capitol Hill at a porch with its mouth hanging open, its windows winking. I parked, taking the key from the ignition, handed it to Brandon. The slamming of car doors echoed in the air.

Inside, we went to the kitchen for water. There were dirty dishes like you wouldn't believe. So we went to the bathroom for a glass of water. Todd began to scrub the bath tub. I watched, unable to draw myself away. I told him it looked pretty clean and he gave me a look like I was crazy and kept scrubbing, then said, "Now, perhaps, it begins to be clean."

"If you think this is bad," Todd's brother was saying, "Once, we all got fascinated by this crack in the bathroom floor. We'd been staring at it forever, when suddenly it was like I saw us from above, from the ceiling, sitting on the floor in a circle in the bathroom staring at this crack. That's when I stopped. When I had stopped, I mean." Moldy shower curtain burned into my mind as I went to the kitchen to search the sink for clean cups. There were bits of melted milkshake and cat food in the bottoms of most of them. "Why did we come to a place like *this*?" Lisa asked. The fact that this was our own apartment hung in the distance. We managed to push it away, finding a bean bag in a corner, where we spent the rest of the night trying to avoid its coming back again.

"Forget the Bible," Todd's brother was saying, "Let's just build a whole new Jesus."

I was supposed to meet Mark in the market for breakfast before work. To little fanfare, a misty sun rose from the roof, where we sat trying not to wake the neighbors.

On the bike ride down the hill, air rushed at my ears, blocking out all other sound. Sunrise at my back, I skidded into the market. I wasn't entirely sure Mark was going to show up, or if I'd come on the right day. Wasn't it the day after the day before? Days only go one by one, one after the other, with nothing but nights between them, so today would be yesterday's tomorrow. Days didn't double up. And the sun was up, so it was day, and it was seven o'clock, so it was morning, and each day only has one morning, so it had to be the right morning of the right day. Then again, it seemed possible I had imagined Mark to begin with. On my person, at the moment, I had, after all, no photo, no token, no physical proof he existed.

There was only one market downtown, though, with only three street corners, and only one with a restaurant. Surely they wouldn't have changed the street name or the restaurant since yesterday. They took orders at the bar. A bored barista poured out rank coffee, adding "Irish Cream" mixer into it. The booths were padded naugahide, jade and maroon. I sat back watching soccer matches on a monitor, snagging ice cubes from the breakfast buffet to kill my nausea. Mark slid into the booth at seven thirty, exactly on time.

I took his hand. It was balled into a fist, so I took it like that, folding my own hand over the fist. I didn't care who looked, the men at the bar, the panhandlers at the door, the waitress, the tourists with morning planes to catch. When I blinked, I saw moldy shower curtains and kitchen sinks overflowing with plastic cups from fast food restaurants' packaged theme meals. The first thing that came into my head was, "I love you."

In the light from the window, watching the expression on his face, I saw this was something he hadn't heard before.

"Then you should move in with me," he said.

He left for work. I stood in the park watching the bay, hands in my pockets to keep them warm, feeling for the twenty I'd brought for breakfast—still there. Turning my back to the water, across the market I could see the top of Mark's office building, pick out his floor in the blue glass. In a wave of happy irony, I told myself I was safe. Nothing, William Haller wrote, glossing Milton, is more indicative of a graceless state than a sense of security, but that's what I felt, standing over the waterfront. This world of things sat at a polite distance. Whatever I'd meant by those three words, I'd said them. I stopped at a florist's. I had in mind a rose, a white one. I had them deliver it to Mark's office.

There was something in the air at the courier base that morning. Something palpable, coming in at the door, a sort of cold panicked distance in the people moving back and forth between the lockers and assignment counter. Someone had been hit. The seconds slowed. Everyone swam through Vaseline as I stood at the assignment counter to hear who.

Todd, flying down Pine Street half an hour before me, had been hit by a Grayline tour bus at an intersection. Seattle's downtown streets were usually empty at that hour. He hadn't stopped at a traffic light.

A Room with a View

Mark's office had a tremendous view of Puget Sound. He watched snow falling across the Kitsap Peninsula on cold days, the rows of piers ranging along the waterfront toward Harbor Island, with their enormous silent orange cranes unloading ships. For nine hours a day he sat in a chair facing the same direction his ancestors had put their faces toward, marching off from the other coast a hundred years earlier. Fifty stories below stretched the last five blocks of distance from the waterfront, the only view invisible from his desk. Whatever energy had led his ancestors to cross a continent, fell forests, lay out street signs and telegraph wires, it was still in him. He was up mornings and out by six.

If you craned your head out the spare back room's window, you could see a wedge of the Sound, swallows zipping through the alley toward the lake. Looking up from the lake, the building seemed the highest point on Capitol Hill, wide dark windows soaking up sunlight in the afternoons from its perch on ravines of ivy.

I stayed at his place whole afternoons, into evenings. I stared at the TV, doodling with pencils, testing Lisa's theory that commercials contain subliminal messages, and that by watching and absentmindedly drawing without looking at the page, one might discover what they were putting in your mind.

"Why don't you go up to the cafe and see what's going on for a while?" he asked, dropping some shopping bags by the door and spreading out on the couch with a pile of papers.

I picked up a red and a white crayon, holding them simultaneously in one hand, squinting at a Coke commercial through Mark's reading glasses.

"Here," he said, fishing in his wallet. "I owe you a five from the other night, don't I? Why not go get yourself a latte?"

The door to a bar up the hill hung propped open with a barstool. From the sidewalk you could hear the jingling of a pinball machine. I found myself racking up pinball shots. Someone put a beer in front of me, and as the last ball went past the flippers, I remembered a line from a poem and tried to catch it in my memory. It came back, familiar again. It wasn't a poem at all, but a dream I'd been having lately. It frightened me that I could dream something often enough to know it by heart, but forget it while awake.

Nothing special was happening in the cafe. In a corner, three black and white console TVs were stacked on top of each other playing the Charlie Brown Christmas Special. I was trying not to smoke and the video screen above the pool table showed a closed caption of the weather report. The caption didn't change for about five minutes and it said, "NO GLOVES.>>PNOT BAD."

Along the sidewalk outside, someone's poinsettias were planted, and a rage rose up in me—idiotic, to plant them outside, in the open air, in the middle of winter. Lake Union was lit up, glittering with lights, crowded with dinner cruise boats of people chowing down on roast chicken and salmon with flavored mousses. I wandered back down the hill, watching the last of the dinner boats gliding out into the bay. I'd left my Walkman in the cafe. Pacing back up the hill, I found it again, sitting in the booth untouched.

There was an unnerving intensity in the eyes of a guy pushing a luggage cart of books outside the cafe door. I stood pulling on my gloves. The paperback he held out had on its cover a woman, tinted a light blue, with swirls of what I supposed were tangible bits of divine ecstasy sweeping around her, as she was smiling, evidently having just been enlightened. I'd bought the same book several months ago for a dollar from a boy on a street corner not far away. I thanked the man and said no, I was still working on a copy. He offered me another, this one with a picture of a meditating Buddha. His eyes were full of love or religious fervor, a look not entirely wasted on me. The look said, "Even if you refuse this book from me now, you and I still share a secret, something no one else on this street might ever understand." Which was flattering, if you felt like sharing unspoken secrets with religious fanatics.

"It's on a donation basis."

I smiled and shook my head.

All that walk back down the hill I thought about the look in his eyes, not with a sense of wonder, because I'd seen it before, but with a realization that I might have been a little in love. As the boats passed in and out between the buildings, I thought of the dream that had been lingering creepily in my head as I tried to wake up in the mornings. Lisa'd read a book about a society of people who, among other things, make a point of telling each other their dreams every morning when they first wake up. This was a thing I had. Ever since she told me about it, I'd wanted to talk about my dreams as soon as I woke up, if there was anybody to talk with about them. Lisa, or people staying over, I always wanted to tell them my dreams. Most of them thought it was strange, but they always humored me. Mark would even ask me before I told him. But for the last weeks I hadn't said anything about dreams in the morning, sleeping over at his place. The first one was just a dark space, nothing. After a while there would be a voice calling, asking, *Where is the red rose?* When I didn't answer, it wrote in red script across the dark blinking screen of the dream: *What have you done with it? Where have you put the red rose?* Or I would dream about the eyes I was thinking about as I walked back to his apartment that night.

My Walkman was over my ears as I climbed the stairs to Mark's place, but before I even put the key in the door I could feel the television on. There was that weird static in the headphones that isn't a sound, just the registration of some other electronic device nearby. Mark had left the TV on in the living room. I thought he was asleep, but as I pulled the covers over myself he grabbed me. I could smell beer on his breath.

"I went out tonight while you were gone," he said. "Everyone said what a cute boyfriend I have."

"Who said that?"

"Everyone."

"What, the whole bar? I don't even know anyone there."

"Trent kept saying what a cute boyfriend I have."

"Who?"

"Trenton. Trent was really really drunk. He went on and on about how you were his type. He can talk. God, you're hot."

I felt my face burn. "You, too," I said.

REHEARSAL

It was "couples' night" at the gay men's chorus rehearsal. Mark had mentioned it three times, so after work I rode the bus around for a while and walked to the place. I thought he'd said it was a Jewish reform school, which seemed a weird place for a gay chorus practice, but it turned out to be a Reform Jewish school, which was different, somehow. It was pretty, with glass cabinets full of all kinds of cups and plates and menoras and whatever, but the coolest thing was a quilt over the door of the auditorium, huge, with everything in it from the Old Testament. I sat outside the rehearsal room reading. There was a table with flowers and a bunch of paper hearts all over it. I was the only person there. After a while the singing stopped and this little guy I'd met before saw me and brought me in where Mark was sitting. There was a stack of nametags by his chair, and the little guy told Mark he was going to make a nametag for me. Mark said, "Well, I wouldn't do it till he shows up," and the little guy said, "Oh, I'm sure he'll come," and Mark said, "Oh, I don't know," in a depressed voice. I tapped him on the shoulder. He looked up and saw me. Smiling, he bolted out the door. I followed him.

He was skittish, like one of those dogs that was skittish as a puppy, more confident now, but still a little skittish out of habit. Like the kind of dog weaned around careless people, then raised by a good family, but still used to the motions of wild arms and legs. Anyway, as the chorus took a little break, we walked round the table. I made jokes.

They were mostly youngish, with that earnest-yet-wily "I'm going to grow up one day to sell you a municipal bond" look. One of them talked about opportunities, starting to say, "It's a chance to . . . ," then stopping himself mid-phrase and changing "chance" to "opportunity." Everything was an opportunity, it seemed. If a house fell out of the sky and landed on you, it was an opportunity to reassess your lifestyle. When I called Mark the next day, I heard him using the word himself.

They went back to sing again. The people who came to hear their partners sat in two rows in the back. There were four of us. The other three sat watching for an hour. I sat reading the whole time, resenting the conductor's stops, because it made me lose my place. There was wine and food set up outside the rehearsal room. A guy came up to ask me my name and why I didn't have a nametag, like he was anxious to see if I really belonged there, and I said I wasn't really a nametag kind of person (the nametag Little Guy made me was a valentine card with a grinning train with a caption under my name that said, "I choo-choo-choose you, Valentine!"), but I told him my name. Without missing a beat, he asked me what I did, which by now I ought to have been used to, but my first reaction was to say, "What do I do when *what?*" So I told him I was trying to be a writer, and he started telling me how he edited this trade journal for some business thing he couldn't explain, asking me what kind of writing I did, all fast, like he'd taken a class called "The Ten-Minute Networking Party" on speed. I told him I liked travel writing. He asked where I'd gone and I told him I'd just been to my parents' house, but people like that never want to hear your impressions of a place, they just want to fill in the blanks of some form they keep in their heads. He asked where else I'd been. So I told him I wanted to go to Europe. He asked what my favorite country was—a question I ought to have had a ready answer for—but such a dumb question I resented having to answer. Mark brought someone else over. The trade journal editor disappeared.

The rest of them were cooler than the trade journal editor. They told little stories, and one guy explained how he was going to Amsterdam for the Gay Games, which was a kind of Olympics only for homosexuals which I guessed gay people went to watch. Maybe their families went, too, I didn't know. Mark bought me raffle tickets, but they didn't win anything, so when they started auctioning the flower arrangements he started bidding. The weird thing was, halfway through, I really started to want these flowers. Set up on a high stand over the table, you could tell they were a little stale, but they still smelled nice, a bunch of palm fronds sticking out all around them. Once he bid once or twice, I knew he'd get them no matter what because I'd seen him bid that way before, and he always went just a little too. When he realized he'd already bid ten dollars too much, he went another ten anyway, and I tried to look down into my empty plastic glass of dessert wine so no one would see how excited I was, but no one was watching. Then there was applause, and the manager came up, saying how we didn't have to pay right now, but Mark already had his wallet out and was pulling out the money. The guy Brian, who brought them, was a florist. While he got something to wrap them up with, I took Mark off to a dark part of the room along the back of the place where a long window looked over the lake. I wanted him to see the water. He stared out a while before he could see it. It almost looked like real water, but slower, mercury in the dark, with only moonlight and streetlamps shining on it. Mark said it was creepy. And it was kind of creepy, from the vestibule of a dark synagogue. Home with the flowers, we pulled them out of the bag Brian put them in, finding all the vases in the apartment. It did cheer me up.

Quick 'N Easy Recipe #23
Easy Mini Chocolate Doughnuts

A box of Cheerios (or several)

Hershey's chocolate bars

Vanilla extract

Red wine

Melt the chocolate in a double boiler and pour over Cheerios spread out on a baking sheet.

Douse with wine.

Bake 20 minutes at 200 degrees.

While hot, pour Vanilla over doughnuts. Ignite.

Mark invited me to a Valentine's Day party some of his colleagues were having. The Embassy Suites is a hotel for people who are staying for a while but don't cook much—film crews or managers with firms trying to convince them to relocate. Its façade, planters bedded with winter pansies, was awash with spotlights to keep homeless people at bay. In its lobby, an obsequious uniformed doorman patrolled chairs that were probably comfortable but didn't look it. By the fireplace, a couple of girls in short black skirts sat at the brass fire screen.

The guy I'd locked eyes with once in Café Paradiso

was at the party. Mark made ingratiating small talk. I asked him who'd invited us.

"Trenton," Mark said.

Trenton himself disappeared. We were left alone with silence, an impression something else was going on in the suite's other room. We walked out under the spotlights, the pansies turning their faces blankly up from concrete beds.

Brandon found me outside a hotel hosting one of those benefits with a lawyer himself. He followed me inside, and we jokingly practiced sucking up to millionaires together. Brandon, more serious, was better at it than I was, easing his way through a swath of law firm partners, arranging a lunch date with a fitness center owner, telling amusing stories to a billionaire's mother, all the while somehow within easy reach of the serving tables. I could only manage to listen to a broker go on about his collection of electric trains for twenty minutes before looking for Mark.

When a friend of Lisa's who'd been squatting at our apartment finally found a job and her own first apartment, she threw a housewarming party. Mark sulked that I hadn't invited him. So I did. He thought it wasn't fair of me to keep a secret social life apart from his. He imagined something glamorous and young and edgy. I knew he wouldn't enjoy it. Her studio was on a storage mezzanine with five-foot ceilings, a mattress, stove and sink, in that order, as you came in the door. We sat against the wall, drinking Mountain Dew from cans, passing around a purple bong. Mark was silent as we went down the stairs afterward and silent in the car. But I knew the next time I had an invitation and didn't ask him to come along, he wouldn't sulk.

I cleaned offices at night to pay the rent. It seemed like a job for a writer. Between six in the evening and six in the morning, you could do the work whenever you wanted. I helped myself to tea and milk from the kitchen. I was moving to clean when the door opened and three employees strode in laughing hysterically. The woman laughed spasmodically for five straight minutes while walking around the desks. One man went into an office with her. The other rifled in his desk, staring at me. I knew who they were because I cleaned their desks. The man kept an Undergear catalog in his top drawer. The woman had a plaque reading "Office Princess." They left together, Undergear guy looking over his shoulder at me like a kid being dragged from an FAO Schwartz window. The whole thing put me in a bad mood.

Sidney Spit

That summer, Mark's lawyer friend Greg, who Brandon seemed to be dating, invited us sailing for ten days.

In the last straggling weeks of a newspaper internship, cleaning offices nights to pay rent, I was spending more and more days drinking coffee across the street from the newspaper. The editors, when they wanted me, were used to crossing the street to find me surrounded by sticky rings of drying coffee at one of the cafe's dozen unwieldy tables. When Greg invited us sailing I gave a week's notice. Our lease was up at the end of the month. Lisa had been swearing she was going to find a new place for weeks. I started slowly moving my things into Mark's.

Brandon, Greg, Mark, Trenton and I met for darts.

"You're not that crazy about darts," I said, sitting at the bar.

"Rather just drink," Brandon said. "Greg gets pissed if I don't play seriously and I hate playing seriously.

"*You're* not that crazy about darts either," Brandon added accusingly.

"Sure I am."

He smiled.

"Game time, boys," Trenton called from over the faces

at the bar, holding up a dart in each hand, pinched between his fingers. I'd recognized the voice as unmistakably *his* over the bar's other voices, surprised I saw his gestures as familiar. Brandon and I took our drinks and pushed through the crowd.

I met Mark for dinner on Broadway in a dark red cafe with too many mirrors and too many desserts. It had begun sprinkling as I got there. He stood under the awning in his suit. We sat by a plate glass window, sunlight growing pale with the rain, reflected back and forth between the mirrors, making our forks and glasses sparkle. I felt neurotic even before the food came, a vague dizziness that wasn't dizziness, an unease that ought to have been in the stomach, but wasn't quite in the stomach.

"What are you thinking about?" I asked.

"Work," he said, eyes coming back from wherever they'd been. Then, more apologetically, "Sorry." The waiter pushed salads onto the table, then moved behind the bar. "We're invited to go out with everyone from the boat for drinks after this," he said.

"You go," I said, feeling suddenly as if I'd lost my land legs, "There's something wrong with my stomach." He passed me the key to his apartment.

They were already coming down the sidewalk toward us at the cafe's door, absorbing Mark, then turning to wander to the end of Broadway and back down the hill. I was grateful for the cool of the slowing rain, the silence it wrapped around the blocks, dampening the sounds of rising or descending cars.

Inside his building's stairwell, quiet light penetrated the mute, still colors of the carpet. It was still too early for bed. I stretched out across the bedspread anyway. Sometime later, light fading through the window blinds, my stomach jolted. I woke with a start. Somebody'd shoved me toward the edge of the mattress. As my eyes opened the picture on the wall was swinging slightly, teetering in a precise geometric arc from its hook, back and forth along the wall plaster.

Mark stepped into the hall. I pulled myself up. We brushed our teeth and climbed back into bed. He turned on the television. There'd been an earthquake. Nothing had happened, really. A few bricks had fallen from a municipal library, no injuries. The news team would work around the clock to keep us informed of other incidents.

Mark was in the middle of trial the week we set sail, his case teetering toward settlement till both sides suddenly pounced into jury selection with such a rage that there was no way out for him until it was all over. Mark held to Greg's sailing invitation in hope. One of the partners let him off for a long weekend so he could make the start of the trip with us, but not all of it. To make up the missing man (Brandon not being much of a sailor),

Trent would be in Victoria for the Swiftsure race and could join us there afterward to replace Mark. I'd continue with the three of them.

Lisa, after months of delay, finally found an apartment further down the hill. Ours was empty, so on the first hot day of summer I dragged my bed to the alley, left our keys with the landlady, and walked down the hill with the last of my stuff to Mark's. Before I'd finished unpacking in Mark's spare room half an hour later, Brandon rang the bell below in Greg's jeep to take me to the marina. We loaded my bag in with his groceries, riding down Denny Way straight into the line of cars inevitably stretching from Capitol Hill to the Space Needle on summer Friday afternoons at the first hint of sun.

"You'll like the boat," Brandon said. "It's spotless. I've been cleaning it all week."

"You've been on it?"

"I've been living on it. The people at the marina don't like it if you sleep there. It'll be nice to leave the lights on after dark for a change, once we're out."

Warmed by the sun, bored at the bottom of the hill, Brandon cut onto a side road toward Ballard. The jeep jolted along Market Street through a haze of shoppers and blue-haired fishermen's wives squinting through their glasses at the astonishing sun.

"Careful," he said, ashing cigarette out the window, then handing it to me. Between us a twelve-pack of mini-vodkas baked by the gear shift. "Don't drop this. With all the alcohol in here we'll be roasted alive in seconds. Greg had me do a liquor store run. You wouldn't believe how much cheaper it is here than in Canada."

He rattled around between bottles in the backseat at a stoplight, reaching for something that had slid, pulling up a lurid red bottle of cherry cordial wrapped in red cellophane. "The label was so kitsch I couldn't resist," he said. "Save it for your first night back in Seattle. Happy housewarming, for you and Mark." From behind the seat, he fished out a bottle of Jägermiester by its black neck, passing it to me. "This one you save for emergencies." Pulling into the marina, he set both in my lap.

Mark had driven straight from the office with as much beer as was allowed across the Canadian border. Brandon and I pulled in mooring buoys. Downtown's skyscraper tops sank behind the band of shore as we motored into the Sound. Greg and Mark talked lawspeak in the cockpit. At dusk, we moored off Port Townsend to make dinner tired, damp, and satisfied, watching the restaurant balconies' candlelight, the sounds of their silverware clanking across the water. Mark and I slept with all our stuff in the V-berth.

We woke to quiet, somber fog. Greg on deck, brown as a latte and intent on deepening his tan, shirt off, covered in goosebumps, crouched over the map, sipping his second beer.

Around noon the rain stopped. The wind picked up. The sun came out and warmed us. Brandon slathered himself in sunscreen. Greg let me sail. Halfway to Victoria three dolphins rose alongside the boat, plowing the water's wake on both sides, taking dives beneath us, disappearing under the bow, resurfacing on opposite sides, smooth, glistening black and white, cutting the water with more force than the wind cut our sails. Lawspeak ceased. We rode at seven knots, leaning into the side of the deck, shivering and smiling behind sunglasses. After an hour of open water, Victoria's sea wall came up, and we followed it as far as the breeze carried. Motoring through the bay, the city closed around us, alive in miniature on every side under the blue sky.

It was hot and breezy on the planks of the marina's dock, spackled with bits of tar, soft under our shoes, while they searched the boat at customs. The sky was a golden blue. Boats from the Swiftsure race had taken most of the mooring spaces. We motored through the marina till we saw Trenton waving from the wall above the bay, running down toward us. Greg pulled in as he directed us, mooring alongside Trent's team's boat. Its boom had bent nearly in half during the race and most of the crew had turned back early, so Trent had been waiting for us.

Trent leaped to our boat before we were within ten feet of the dock, pulling us in by our rigging wires while

Greg scolded, "If everyone on your boat pulls on things that way it's no wonder the boom is bent." Trent ignored him, taking mooring buoys from me as I handed them to him, one after another, tying them as neatly as you please, paying no attention to Greg, Brandon, Mark or myself. He and Greg stood comparing tans, each stretching out a forearm and pressing them together, pointing out other boats from the race around us, masts jingling lightly each time a sea plane took off from the bay. Someone handed Trenton a drink and he stood there, tan in his ridiculous plaid shorts, red cap, and blue Oxford and prescription sunglasses, avoiding my gaze. It was lawspeak again. I leaned back, closing my eyes, pretending to listen. They might as well have been speaking another language.

By now, there were two thin pale Victoria boys and a girl in a navy captain's jacket and a blue skirt on deck. "The girl's transgendered," Brandon whispered, once he was close enough to say something. "And she has a glass eye," he said. He'd stashed away about a six-month supply of liquor between the life jackets.

There was a party somewhere, evidently, that night. There was chuckling on deck while Brandon made drinks in the cabin. The sun grew fainter. The breeze cooled in the mild buzz from the cocktails Brandon kept bringing up into the endless flow of legal terms. Even with my eyes closed I could tell Mark was drunk; whenever he said something his words came in little bursts, as if he were spitting. After a while it was colder, and the only thing warm on deck was Mark's side and his shirt, the muscles of his shoulder tensing a little each time he spoke. After a while, he seemed to hurry his phrases, as the low boom of Trenton's voice broke everything else off. There were no pauses when Trent spoke. His voice continued in the spaces between words and phrases, a low drawling growl. My preference for it, even half asleep, felt vaguely disloyal.

The girl in the captain's jacket cocked her head to look at her watch. She probably wasn't transgendered at all, and for the rest of the night we all tried to figure out who had started the rumor, but never did.

Come on, said Trent, once everything on the boat had been silent for a long while, his voice close in my ear. *Do you want to get something to eat?* I opened my eyes and saw everyone else waiting on the dock. Trent leaped from the boat, holding a hand out to me.

"Ian, you'd better take a sweater," Mark called from the dock. I pulled one over my head as we climbed the seawall stairs. I had that strange, uneasy feeling you get after napping in the evening when you wake up cold, and smoking a cigarette seems to take all the remaining warmth out of you, and your legs walk, feeling nothing but just go on.

Trenton left us on the main street to say goodbye to

the rest of his crew, then met us in a dark room with too many salt shakers and a disconcerting number of ice cream flavors. He sat across from me between Mark and Greg, holding his wine glass—everything he held was always his—over a green check table cloth, the empty plate before him clean enough to reflect the sheen of his hair. What he was saying was funny. Even the waiter was listening. In fact everyone was listening, his Oxford collar casting a bluish light on the underside of his chin. An invisible something fluttered now and then in Mark's hands, showing nowhere in his face. It was all lawspeak again. Cases and cases. I'd heard enough of these stories; they're rarely funny. His wine glass glowed in front of a candle. Trenton looked into space, frowning at nothing. He and Mark took patient turns talking, frowning and looking away as the other talked. This was one of those lawyer's tricks I'd seen in Mark's textbooks. Frown while the other side is presenting their case.

It flashed through my mind that I should have done anything, made any arrangement or excuse to see they'd been seated at opposite ends of the table or, at any rate, that I wasn't seated across from both of them. The thought flashed through my mind that if the world were mine and there were no feelings or objects, possessions or friendships in it, now, and now, and now, at this juncture or that, I would leap across the table to him.

We went to a bar to drink ciders and play darts.

Canadian money was play money for Americans—a dollar was only fifty cents or something, so even if you couldn't keep the exchange rate in mind, you had the sense of spending less than you imagined. Add to this that you were dispensing it to English speakers, which took away from the ominous sense in places where transactions are half-understood—where you smile, and they smile, and perhaps neither of you is ever sure who is exploiting whom. You ended up feeling sorry for Canadians who bought you drinks, and they felt the absurdity of the situation, too, yet it would be absurd to visit Canada and buy two rounds for every Canadian who bought you one.

Mark and I drank ciders, watching what appeared to be teenagers playing pool. There seemed to be two bars in Victoria. Both served cider. One you reached by going down a set of stairs to a basement. The other you reached by going upstairs to the second floor. We went to one, then the other, then back again, before we ran into Trent. We threw darts, marking the chalkboard, which, with the real non-computer-assisted cork dartboard, fascinated everyone. The cider was cold to the touch, then warmed, sweeter and stickier as you drank. Someone kept handing me full bottles until I had three of them lined up on a shelf behind me. They came in three flavors—Washington Red, Granny Smith, and Pear. Two Granny Smiths in a row made your stomach twist. Two rounds of Washington Red left your mouth sticky with sugar. Pear ran out after the first three rounds. I alternated between the former, ending up with a slight but constant abdominal cramp and wanting to brush my teeth. Leaving Brandon leaned against a wall in the corner, I walked off to dance. I was dancing like crazy. Trent sat alone, very still on a stool in the corner, drinking his cider. Then we were dancing, the only ones on the floor, pulling on shirts again as soon as we were reasonably cool afterward. The bar was closing and we were going to a party somewhere in someone's car. There were still people on the street outside, but the Americans were the only ones making any noise. The Canadians talked. The rest of us shouted, carrying each other down the sidewalks.

"No, no," someone said from the front seat. "I don't care about that. I just want something to happen tonight. Something's going to happen, isn't it?"

"No worries," a voice answered. We stopped at a red light. A pair of faces peered back at the five of us pushed together against the vinyl in the back of the car. The girl rumored to be transsexual sat in front of me, hand out the window, holding a cigarette, carefully holding the smoke away from me. I was holding a bag of tofu wieners on my lap, with another bag of hamburger buns between my feet which I was trying to remember not to crush. "Are you all right?" someone asked, and I leaned back, smiling at whoever it was.

The house was the big sprawling kind Californians were fond of building in the sixties in a suburb of low wide houses, lights on in every room, all the ceilings of a uniform lowness stretched above carpeted spaces blank as the ceilings, furniture packed in the edges and corners. Brandon and I danced. Someone watched from a couch with an amused grin. Outside, a deck, a gas grill that wouldn't start, a translucent pool lit blue from below. Inside, the girl broke a glass and everyone reassured her it was all right. Mustard and tofu and drinks with strawberries that didn't quite turn out right. There was some boy who kept ferrying people back and forth to Victoria. There was a model ship in a bottle on a mantle. I was wearing someone else's sweater with the uneasy feeling that the someone was watching to see that I didn't leave with it, though I couldn't remember who'd given it to me.

Greg dove into the pool. Brandon sat in a deck chair, pants around his ankles, watching the water and shivering. We went inside to sit on a couch for a while between an oil painting of a raccoon fishing in a blue creek and another of a bowl of fruit. In the kitchen was a cooler of beers, and when I asked for one someone almost poured it down my throat for me. I kept finding myself in that empty living room with its dead silence and glassed-in boat, then wandering out again around the pool. Each time I went back to the kitchen everyone smiled as if I'd been gone a long time, so I'd stay until I'd decently finished my beer, and each time I came back Brandon was sitting on the floor waiting for my turn in the Trivial Pursuit game he'd laid out, as if I hadn't been gone long at all. Finally, Brandon was no longer there, the game alone splayed across the carpet of the empty room. There was shouting from the open doors. I saw movement outside. Greg, still damp from his swim, sat on a deck chair, while Brandon stood over him shouting obscenities, then turned to me, pulling me inside. I stood by the fireplace with Brandon while he shouted lines from *Pulp Fiction*, and kept shouting them all night, even after a cab took us back to the boat very early in the morning, half his body visible in the hatch, glass in hand, the marina's race flags quivering in the air around us, ropes and gear clanking against a sea of masts.

Mark took the Victoria clipper back to Seattle the next morning to finish his case. I walked him to the dock, then followed the bay's edge in the heat for a while, not eager to get back to the boat.

Victoria's eastern edge is all semi-gated condominiums with views, dry weedy stretches of grass and monuments between them, surrounded by strange, tough-looking trees clipped around their bases. A string of cars pulled out of one condo's concrete porte-cochère, filed off in a row around its side, and disappeared. I walked out on the seawall, scraping gravel from my shoe soles against its ledge, the only audible sound, the broad stretching city laid in pieces in front of me, the green and blue hills and sky above it. Gradually I heard the sound of the gravel I was grinding under my shoes, and it was finally then I realized I was alone. The silence hit me. I was waiting to miss Mark, and the feeling came after a while. It sometimes takes moments before you can miss someone. *It takes this*, I thought, waiting with the sound until my arms felt empty. I'd felt their emptiness the same way I'd realized the sound of the stones scraping, slowly, the body's urge to hold something that will hold it back. All that water, I thought, on the ocean, and people pressed together so closely there on the land and, beyond the Haro Strait, more wide empty land, with elk and rabbit that have never seen a human face. A truck driving through it might dent that silence for a minute as it passed, then be gone again, leaving anyone listening thinking they'd imagined it.

I'd seen wildlife documentaries of some wide empty plain where animals, coming up from their holes into a silent world, look around with something appearing, onscreen, like reverence. When, in the course of the animal sagas they enact between dandruff shampoo and life insurance commercials, one of the animals leaps up on awkward hind legs, letting out a cry into that silence, they cut it short midway to look around, their furry jowls as horrified and apologetic as an actor who has just spoken his lines badly. Maybe it's an echo that frightens, but I think it's more the realization that silence, which undisturbed seems the strongest force in the universe, is so easily broken, and takes a moment to repair itself. They stand stiff on their legs, listening and waiting.

I circled the bay on the dry road back to the parliament building, set back from the wharf like an aristocrat too polite to notice the crowds milling at its base. A few sailboats moved off across the bay, heading back to Vancouver after the race. I realized I'd walked around all morning more to avoid going back than for anything else.

In the BC Museum were rock carvings "from before the time when animals became men."

Do the opposite of what you want, I told myself, sitting outside the museum's cafe. *Sit here with your coffee and your cigarette in the sun, taking a sip of coffee every time you want a drag from your cigarette, and every time you want a sip of coffee, take a drag from your cigarette.*

Trenton showed up, tossed his bag into the hold, and we pulled out, following Swiftsure's departing boats, then broke off east to head for Sidney Island. There was a stretch of quiet on the water again after the weekend of music and strained voices. Looking at my watch, I tried not to imagine someone walking across an over-bright room, onto an over-bright lawn, bending to pick empty martini glasses from the grass around the edge of a pool. The eastern suburbs' bluffs spread alongside us in bright white points; we hoisted the sail. I went below deck and stretched out by my bag in the V-berth. Through the cabin's open door, Greg and Trent were talking on deck. Greg's voice had an impertinent questioning lilt. Trent was saying, "We drove back after you all left, and I told him as soon as my head hit the pillow I was asleep, so we sat in the car in front of my hotel for a while and then I went to bed."

Greg snickered. "And what did you do in the car?"

"I don't kiss and tell."

"God, why are you so squeamish about details?"

Trent came down into the hold, nodding at me through the cabin door.

Everyone was trying to be healthy, but drinking a six-pack of cider a day and a bottle of wine, smoking those damned Canadian cigarettes with their blatant warning labels.

Sidney Spit is a long yellow arm of sand with a green island at its far end. Walking the kilometer or so down it, over logs and driftwood piled on the high side of the beach, you assume you'll find another island on the other side. But there's nothing at the end of the spit. A spit is a beach just leading to more beach.

We moored offshore where some buoys floated, Greg taking off alone in the kayak, leaving Trent, Brandon and me to pump up the dingy to explore the island. The dingy sprang a leak and was full of water by the time we reached the beach and dragged in into the driftwood. Trent stood, his knees blue from the cold. The island was deserted. Brandon and I ran through the forest to the cliff to throw stones at the beach below, taking bigger and bigger rocks, hoisting a fallen tree from either side to watch it plunge to the shore, then walked down to the beach to see where it had fallen. Brandon walked out to the spit to sun himself and nap. The path to the beach led to a long mowed lawn where deer came to sniff at biscuits left by boaters. *Tell me what movies you like*, Trent said. I felt a kind of land-sickness, with the sensation I was going to reel off the sand into the water. The bay was deep and clear with views of the sandbars beneath. He was making conversation gently, evenly, earnestly curious but with a manner as if we'd already talked many times before, a studied casualness, and after anything I said he had some amusing story which made my own comment sound reasonable.

Tell me what books you like, he said.

Moving out of sight of Brandon, we sat on the spit looking out at the boat. Once the conversation lapsed, we immediately took, each of us at once, the hand of the other. A simple, impossible, ridiculous gesture, fulfilling like the first breath on the surface after a plunge under-water. The patch of grass we stretched out on bloomed bright green, as if illuminated by a different sun.

The grass is always greener on the other side, he was saying.

Meaning what? I asked.

Meaning . . . He mused for a minute as if, like my hand in his, this, too, ought to be wordlessly understood. *Would you be doing this if you weren't with Mark?*

I laughed. *I don't know. Probably? I think so. Would you?* It was the first and last time we both laughed.

"Maybe not," he said, rolling over away from me on the grass.

He turned his head back again. "That was harsh, wasn't it?" he murmured.

"It's okay," I said. There was so little we shared at the moment that it seemed urgent, imperative, every gesture, word, phrase, movement signal a bond. He sat up stiffly as Greg's kayak passed along the shore, moving toward the boat. I lay still, looking at the sky.

"There's a thing about wanting what you can't have, though," he said.

"So we'll keep the grass green," I said. The fabric of his shirt was washed warm by the sunburn beneath it. We lay like that for a while. Then he gave me a push and a grin and we sat up, taking each other's hands, feeling the joints and the nails and the calluses. There was nothing else to do. The wind died. He whitened his nose with my sunscreen, poring over his *Vanity Fair*. I sweated.

A line of driftwood and shrubs straddled either side of the spit and we walked on this until the scruffiest grasses bruised the bottoms of our feet. Brandon was nowhere to be found. We rowed back in the dingy, poking in the cabinets for something to drink. There was a bottle of champagne. Eight ciders were chilling in the cold box for dinner. In the bread cabinet we found Brandon's bottle of cherry liquor.

Trent lifted it up to the light from the hatch, squinting narrowly at the gold label. Each time his arm came toward mine I could feel its outline radiating heat like an aura.

"My god. I can't believe Gregory drinks this stuff."

"He doesn't. Brandon gave it to me."

He turned the lid, snapping it open to tear the seal. "My god, look at this lurid label. We should keep it as a souvenir. Put it in your scrap book." It poured into glasses like bloody syrup. We carried them up and leaned against the mast. "You're moving in with him?"

"It's done," I said. He lifted the bottle again to our glasses, then to his mouth, then to mine, till it was empty, and tossed it into the bay.

The sky. His neck close to my ear. Hearing his breath and knowing he was sitting quiet listening to my breath. When we heard Greg and Brandon coming up, I felt

Trent suddenly awake, but knew his eyes would still be closed. He was listening to my breathing again now, as I was to his, each of us listening to the other's reaction.

From the deck that night, we watched deer on shore, coming out from the trees onto the cliffs to look at us. The four of us sat on deck playing Monopoly. Brandon was out after four turns. All of us were out finally, except Trent. I made dinner. Trent stretched out on the seats by the door of the V-berth, reading *Vanity Fair*. No one said anything to him, and he didn't look up. "Do you want to camp?" I asked. I'd brought a tent.

He looked up from his magazine with an uncertain smile. "Maybe. That might be fun. Do I have to decide right now?" Greg sat by the lamp folding maps at the table. I put some more air in the dingy and rowed out to the shore, found a level place along the cliffs and set up the tent. There were raccoons on the island, fussing in the bushes, coming out to look at my campfire. I could hear the three of them on the boat, their voices echoing across the water's surface. At some point, Trent called my name, joking, his voice breaking and hoarse with effort.

Greg and Brandon were on deck drinking coffee as I rowed back the next morning. Trent was crouched over the table in the hold, his face dark as he looked up into mine. His eyes flashed, his lips turning down. Without a word, he stood and the two of us went up to pull off the sail cover. The sail rose, tremored, shook, blew out full, then went silent as the prow slashed the water before us in two.

The sun cleared as the bow nosed into the edge of the Gulf Islands. We found Roche Harbor by dinner time, trees slanting down the hills toward the bay as if pushing each other from behind to get down to the water, impeded here and there by glass-fronted mansions glinting red and gold, hanging from the cliffs along the harbor's sides.

"I could live there," Trent said, pointing to one of the less extravagant palaces blocking the trees' fall the shore. "I had a boyfriend once, a law student at the U. I always thought of us living in a place like that, running a firm together with faxes and teleconferences, and never having to leave it."

"Mmm," I said.

"I'd still like to. I still call him. Whenever I get excited about a case or something, he's the person I call. I don't know if we could ever be . . . happy." He paused, looked out, then back at me, his eyes going up and down my face.

The hilltops around the bay glowed like back-lit jade. The resort and its dining room's terrace glinted sun into our eyes, the landing below dotted with roses and white-washed arbors. "I've been here before," Brandon said, as Greg walked up to look at the menu and we stood on the deck. "This guy I used to date always took me in a plane to the airfield, then they have a limousine that takes you to the hotel. Whenever I asked him how old he was he always said sixty-nine with this really cheesy dirty laugh." Brandon knew the restaurant, too. I pulled on a clean shirt I'd slipped in the dry cleaning bag with Mark's things the week before. I slicked back my hair with water from the sink.

Greg came back. "They have a good vegetarian dish. I think we can make it for under twenty each with drinks."

I followed the others along the sunbaked planks of the dock, Trent's brown calves moving in front of me. We thought about a drink in the bar downstairs, but were all too hungry to bother waiting. Trent smiled at the bartender, heading up the stairs to the restaurant, taking them two at a time. The staircase, narrow, turned at a funny angle. The dining room's west windows overlooked the harbor, and as I came out of the stairwell, the glare left Trent a black silhouette like a heavy shadow before me. I stepped toward him. My foot hit something. Then I was falling, at first into nothing—then my palm contacted the cool, smooth surface of a table top briefly, before going through it. There was the sound of shattering glass, then of solid chunks of thick glass hitting the floor with a heavy, reverberating thud.

Now dinner will be screwed, I thought.

I was pulled roughly up from behind. My knees stung.

Blood beaded on them, and pooled in my hands. Trent led me down the hall to a bathroom, wiping my cuts, pulling the glass from them. The blood seemed unnaturally dark. The bathroom was narrow, papered with red roses, Edwardian style, delicately painted with thorns and overlapping petals in shades of red and pink. "Are you okay?" Trent was saying. His eyes were blue and sharp, appraising as he looked at me. I tried to meet them with an equal clarity. He grinned.

Someone else said, "He's in shock."

"Are they deep?"

"Just on my finger," I said. "It's split open." Trent looked at it, grabbing paper towels and handing them to me, then wiping at the floor, spotted with pools of blood.

With two other men in the room it was suddenly full and busy. One seemed to be the restaurant's owner. The other carried a fist aid kit—"Do you have any sharp pains, like glass still in the wounds?"

"No, I think I got it all out."

"Okay, let's start bandaging them up." The man pulled a latex glove over his right hand. "I'm going to put some Neosporin on them."

Trent finished wiping the blood from the floor and put his hand on my shoulder like a benediction before squeezing out the door. "We'll be at the table," he said.

"This is the worst one," said one man.

"You'll need stitches in that one, I think," said the restaurant's owner, a big man with blue eyes, who looked like he would ordinarily have been a jolly guy. The other man, as he held the first aid kit, was busily patching up the cuts. "Here, hold this one, give it pressure," he said, until he had worked his way around it.

"What happened?" I asked.

"You must not have seen the table when you came in. The top of the table was glass. You fell through it. Yeah. Looks like you'll need a couple of stitches in this one."

"I don't want to go into town," I said. From the map, it looked like a long cab ride each way. I couldn't remember if I had insurance that month. The men looked at each other. "I don't care if it scars," I said.

The restaurant owner stared at me a minute, looking for shock or bravado or perhaps just a tendency to sue, but I kept my eyes clear, and knew what a butterfly bandage was, and the restaurant owner wasn't sure himself. The man with the first aid kit warned me to clean it and change it. "Take it to a clinic as soon as you can. Where will you be tomorrow?"

"Sucia."

"No clinic there. Well, keep it clean. And make sure that bleeding stops."

"Here," said the other man, "Let's wipe up that sink." He'd taken off his gloves. The room had the kind of musty cleanness of the washroom in a country club. The roses in the wallpaper had burned themselves into my eyes by the time I got to the dining room. When I blinked, I saw roses.

Someone called. "Ian! Over here." A waitress was standing over the table. "Are you okay?" It was Brandon.

"Maybe I'm not used to land yet. I'll have a beer. Whatever you're having." Pulling my hand from the table, it left a spot of blood on the tablecloth. I pulled Trent's bread plate over it.

We finished our beers.

"You look like you need a cigarette," Greg said. "I know I do. You scared me."

"You give me a call when we get back if that doesn't heal. Permanent nerve damage—serious law suit there," Trent said with a laugh. "Let's all smoke. We'll take turns. You and Greg go first."

There was no trace of the table at the head of the stairs now—someone had taken it away and swept up the glass.

Outside, a terraced garden stretched with beds of orange poppies, a trellis over the path covered in blooming roses, the balustrade warm with the day's sunshine. My knees were bleeding a little again.

Greg didn't have Trent or Brandon's empathetic camaraderie. He was nervous someone from his crew had tripped and fallen, sober, on dry land. I was probably seeming like a cumbersome piece of furniture left in his care, now that Mark had taken the clipper back to Seattle, a cargo to be hauled through the islands. Greg talked only of the flowers as we stood by the orange poppies, and when I asked him where we'd sail the next day it was to give him something to talk about more than because I cared. "We'll go to Stuart Island next," he said, "Spend a few days there, then go on to Friday Harbor."

Brandon had cultivated this new shit-eating grin he was beginning to practice. His short, pleasant laugh followed most things he or Greg said. But when he and Trent came in from their smoke in the garden laughing together I felt—almost jealousy. No one was very hungry by then. We went downstairs to the bar and ordered drinks, which none of us finished. It was dark by the time we got back to the boat. Once Greg and Brandon had gone to bed, Trent laid sheets out for himself in the main cabin, then came into the V-berth to sit on the edge of the mattress. I closed my eyes, lying very still.

"Okay?" he asked.

"Yeah, fine."

"You sure?"

"Yeah. Thanks."

He looked at me once more before turning out the light.

"Does it hurt?"

My finger throbbed.

He was still for a long time, until I thought he might have fallen asleep. But with an unsure slur in his voice, sounding partly like a laugh, said, "We have to talk." His face was very close. With the light through the hatch above I could see the outline of his head.

"Go ahead," I said.

"The first time I saw you was in that cafe. You looked at me. Then at that office."

"Yes."

"You were at that party at that hotel with Mark."

"We didn't know anyone there but you. And no one we asked knew who you were."

"I caught your eye as I came in."

Lately, I'd noticed I talked when I should let someone else talk, and fell quiet when I should have been saying something. I could think of a thousand things to say, so decided to shut up.

". . . Since then," Trent was saying, rolling back away from me into the dark. "I don't know where this is going."

Something one of us hadn't thought of would make it reasonable for me to roll toward him, I thought. For a minute I was sure I was on the verge of rationalizing a logic for touching him, and it was with shock and disappointment at the world's flatness that, as my thoughts spun out, I saw there wasn't one.

"I don't know Mark that well, but I have a lot of respect for him," Trent was saying.

"Yeah." I closed my eyes. "I don't keep secrets from him."

We lay there like that in the dark, until his presence

wasn't something on the other side of the mattress, but the dark itself around us. "There's no way this can happen," he said, loud, strangled as the last syllable caught in his throat. This assertion intoned into the dark, with nothing more to say, everything was easier. He rolled away, leaving a single long strip of my skin against his. Holding his fingers, one at a time, I felt their warmth, until each of our fingers was exactly the same warmth. It was a relief, like breathing air after holding your breath. We slept.

A single drop of water formed across the top center of the berth, rolling slowly, dropping about once every hour. The door to the berth swung closed in the night. Early in the morning, light coming through the hatch, Trent rose to pull it open again. We rolled apart as Greg came to start the coffee, each of us holding a palm to the space in the mattress's center, the warm spot ebbing up from the sheet to the air of the cabin. We got up, downing our coffee, hoisting the sail, as the prow slit the water.

He smiled a cautious smile that afternoon from time to time, pulling himself up on deck after lunch, ramming his shoulder into mine so our chests nearly touched. His hair had shocks of hallucinatory blue, like characters in comic books sometimes have. The silhouette of his face, the rim of his cap against the sun, his cheek. I caught the hint of his breath. Taking me by the shoulder, digging his fingers through the grain of my sweater, he kneaded it, pulling at the wool. "You come from money, don't you?" he growled quietly.

I lied automatically, without thinking, wanting to please him on at least that point, though it was, either way, the wrong answer.

The boat bumped a wave. His shoulder knocked mine again. We watched the bow slash the water.

Slowing off Stuart Island as a fog rolled in, Greg, invisible at the prow, blew a fog-horn every twenty minutes. In the harbor, the fog rolled up across the deck. Twin banks of the inlet's mouth reached though the incredible fog—two dinosaur heads, grazing mouths. Seagulls appeared mid-flight from the dock. A rain drizzled. Greg stretched a tarp over the cockpit, where raindrops still ran with occasional thlunks into our drinks. Moving to the prow, I watched four fingers stuck out of the V-birth hatch, brown, drumming slowly on the edge of the hatch.

The inlet was silent, a silence carried on the water, the whole bay's silence carried across to us. I pulled up the hatch where his fingers drummed. His hand caught my knee, pressing, cold, into the flesh around it. I had an epiphany: despite him, I was drawn dumbly to him, in a dumb, mute, blind search for something beneath his skin, something in his bones, in his breath's pull and outtake.

We motored for an hour, on the bow calling out for floating logs, sounding the foghorn, and docked on Orcas Island, climbed to a resort to sit in a hot tub for two hours, showered, then dried our shoes at the heater, napped. The light, clear, white light, filtered through clouds, like grow-lights, shone blue on his skin.

We reached Friday Harbor, the sun high. I walked with Trent down the boardwalk, alone among the crowd, with the thrill you get from time alone with a favorite grandparent. He shopped, the skin of his arm dark on the counters of a half dozen shops, bought a coffee pot for Greg, a glass bottle of shells for Brandon, then suddenly announced he'd booked a seat on the seaplane service back to Seattle that evening.

Greg wasn't happy at Trent's sudden unplanned departure. It left three of us on board to sail home alone. We'd sail back the way we'd come instead of going around through Deception Pass and east of Whidbey Island. The sun still high, in his sunglasses and that blue pressed shirt, Trent stood on the dock with me a last minute, then boarded his plane, rising above the harbor, till he was a low speck on the horizon. There was nothing but his cap in our berth, hidden in a tuck of in the bed sheets. I walked back to the boat where Brandon and Greg were waiting. "Dinner?" someone asked. "Yes," I said, still sitting there, waiting as if a moment hadn't come yet. Then remembering there was nothing else to wait for. Brandon baked mussels with tiny olives. There was a forced joviality in dinner that night, and the next, as we pulled into the marina, Mark's headlights beaming up at us from the parking lot.

There's a stillness of air on land, always delicious stepping off a boat when it's chilly after sundown. Mark's face, white in the parking lot's lights, had something missing. He was eager to get my things into the trunk. Brandon and Greg got theirs quickly into Greg's, hardly two words exchanged as we drove off, the light of Greg's jeep illuminating its license tag as it floated out the gate before us into darkness. In the warm, tree-scented land air at the car windows, Mark was saying the same kinds of things he'd said before we left, with the same voice, in the same tones.

Sunburned

Home and sunburned, I hung Trent's cap on the coat rack, unpacking duffel bags in Mark's spare room. I poked around the newspaper office, picking up some books to review, biking the city. Messages from various jobs I'd applied for showed up on the voicemail. My finger, when I pulled up the bandage, was white, the color bleached, numb.

In Mark's apartment, like a child in a museum, I was amused, then bored, full of expansive energy, forever afraid I'd knock over something expensive and break it. I thought about applying to the university. The idea of student loans left me paralyzed. I took out a Peace Corps application, reworking the essay questions, putting it away to forget it, rolling coins from Mark's change box, changing them for coffee, rolls, and cigarettes. Sometimes Mark left the room for a minute and I'd miss him. Two days after his flights to Houston or Los Angeles, around noon, I found myself wishing he were back.

I had this theory you can see a person's life in his eyes. If a person has to work hard or if their life is easy, their eyes will show it. That summer, I watched my own eyes go dim in the mirror each morning. "You can't just sit around the house eating bon bons," Mark said.

I volunteered to tutor Vietnamese refugees at the community college. I applied for a job at a plant store in the market.

The sky turned a vapid blue. It rained every night, foggy till noon when wind, coming up from the Sound, spread the clouds, tattering them to ragged bits, sending them east up the mountains. Afternoons were the bluest part of the day. People on Broadway gazed up as they walked, inadvertently smiling at each other conspiratorially. You took a vacation after quitting a job to find another waiting. Sometimes you lost a vacation in taking a job. Sometimes you lost a job in taking a vacation. It's nice to have a job already lined up. It's also nice not to have any idea what to do next. I pedaled to the furthest-flung coffee shops along Lake Washington.

On a bike, you're that floating, transparent eyeball. By the time anyone catches your gaze, you're gone. I spent days not speaking to anyone at all, watching hundreds, thousands of people. Earlier conversations stuck in my mind between the cushions of silence with the utmost clarity, seeming weirdly symbolic.

Seattle's north waterfront ended in a bike trail wending northwest, past great three-story grain dispensers emptying loads of dusty yellow cereals into boats for Russia in the 80s, when Russia could still pay for them.

A park stretched along the shore, peopled with joggers and lunchers, the Space Needle rising to the east, great boulders piled to break the tides against the shore below the Post-Intelligencer's revolving globe. Half a mile from the wharf, a fishing pier with a snack bar. After this the crowds thinned out. Along an inlet with a microscopic beach, passing another biker, our heads shifted in curiosity behind our mirrored glasses. The trail turned, grafting up the street to Magnolia, dead-ending at a cliff-side marina with tiny beaches. Climbing the hill past the coast guard station, you rolled, with some luck, through Discovery Park, the furthest west you could go inside Seattle. Eagles. Sand cliffs dropping, eroding into the Sound, the wind low from the water, pressing into the cliffs, sent shivers through the underbrush.

Southward, along the industrial wastes of the city's lower side, across the bridge to West Seattle, I haunted one green hill. For a few dollars, you could sit on the deck of a waterfront restaurant among the tie and cellular phone crowd, drinking Perrier or Coke. A marimba band (three bearded guys in Hawaiian shirts) played the theme from *The Flintstones*, watching couples eating lobster. At the peninsula's point, narrow rock walks sheltered double-parked BMWs, then a narrow pine park of old men walking dogs through mists churned up from the water at the ferry terminal. You could take the ferry to Vashon Island, waiting at the dock in the sunset, catching a ferry back downtown, riding up the hill home or meeting Mark at Wild Ginger or the Pink Door. With these two rides, making great circles of the city without losing sight of it, I waited for the phone to ring.

At Broadway's end, climbing First Hill to the International District, at the Danny Woo gardens, I sipped canned soy milk from Uwajimaya, lying on a bench, watching gardeners carry mulch, the eight-story cranes silently shifting caskets of Korean automobiles from incoming ships at the bay's edge, sounds echoing from a heroin dealer barking to passersby at the foot of the hill, the hiss of afternoon traffic. Fog rose, fell. The highway shone, a darkening yellow haze on one of the most scenic and unseismographically-sound viaducts ever conceived. The Pacific Hospital hung above the green hill where squatters built cities of tents and tarps. Beyond ramps and highway cloverleaves, Vietnamese malls towered three stories, bustling with battered Hondas and Nissan Sentras.

The Danny Woo gardens are invisible from below, through trees ripe with cherry blossom. Karaoke caverns gilded with yellow plastic drew in Dim Sum clients and waitresses dropping trays of hot sake onto greasy green tabletops with salutary smiles while businessmen mouthed Madonna lyrics on a tiny stage. On the gardens' hill the air was fresh, the highway roaring by on one side as tankers belched, pulling in to make them-selves easy on the wharf shore. The rest of the valley was where most of the raves and afters had moved in recent months. The week after the sailing trip, a trio of drag queens in ostrich feathers had been denied access to the back of a warehouse, standing in line thirty min-utes for ID checks in the rain. The heroin seller's footsteps shuffled up and down the stones, met with cries of an angry drunk squalling for change, drifting along the gardens' terraces into otherwise empty air. Women turned the soil, hamstrings bent, hair pulled back, leaving an easy sensation over the terraced gar-den. The soymilk, sweet and warm in the sun, left me sleepy. At the hill's crest, below a line of new condos, was a pig-roasting pit where, local rumors had it, dogs from the squatter's camp were roasted after dark. I lay down, staring at the sky.

By four o'clock, downtown a riot of street musicians and portable granita machines, bike messengers hocked loogies through the sunroofs of sports cars stuck in the sudden slog of traffic. By five the last cafe terrace was empty. The mannequins in the windows of Nordstrom struck poses for no one. The weather was excuse enough for most of the workers downtown to take off early, making the migration up the hill toward Broad-way. You could sit in a cafe on Pike or Pine to watch the over-heated parade march up the thirty-degree grade in pinstripes and Rockports, coats slung over shoulders, ties flapping from briefcases. Below, the bay lay blue until seven, then shone violet with traffic fumes till sundown.

BRANDED

It was a lazy week at work. Lana, the Jerry Garcia fan from the boat tours, found me a job at a plant store. She kept fucking up the computer, or it fucked up on Lana. She made it worse by pressing buttons at random. It was sunny by the shop's windows along the sidewalk. I wanted to fix the fountain in the front window in the sun, slowly, to make it work well. But Ken imagined I knew more about computers than Steve, and made me go back and fix it. The printer and the modem were screwed up, too. Lana giggled, jamming all the buttons her fingers could find. She wore a lot of eye shadow. Her daughter had been in to visit her that morning. Lana pressed buttons for a while. I went back out to the floor, knowing I'd have to go back to the printer as soon as she got tired of screwing with it. I stood around smiling at people.

I hated pacing myself. Everyone else in the plant shop seemed to pace themselves better. Still, seeing I got everything done, they didn't seem to care so much that sometimes I didn't do anything. I'd stashed a copy of *Madame Bovary* in the book corner, and wanted to pretend to reshelf books, but Ken had already had that idea. Finally Lana left for lunch, saying I should call Steve to ask him what to do. So I went back and, after pressing all the same buttons Lana had pressed, fixed the printer. Steve, calling in a panic, said, "What's wrong with the printer?" And I said nothing was wrong, really. It was fine, thanks. He seemed disappointed.

Lana came back from lunch, radiant and happy. The doctor said if she wanted more children, she had to do exactly what he said, and that she shouldn't work so hard. She'd been working hard. She sat on a stool at the register and everyone was nice to her. The attention made her glow.

The phone rang from the office. Ken called me to take it. It was Lisa.

"Are we going hiking this weekend?" I said.

"Sure. Sure. But not this weekend. Listen, I decided to get branded."

"Branded?"

"Yeah," she said. "My friends convinced me. Well, one friend. The guy in the movie we saw?"

I vaguely recalled an afternoon we'd spent with a bag of organic tortilla chips watching a videotape of someone having a bull's eye stitched in leather straps to the skin of his back. "The Torture King?"

"Yeah, he's in town. My friend designed this really cool brand for me. Want to come? Tonight. It's a party." She gave an address somewhere near the Space Needle. "It's open," she said, "Just go in." I rode my bike down around eleven.

There wasn't a door at the address. At the end of an alley, a twelve-foot hole in the brick opened to a garage, featuring a taxidermied cat under a spotlight. From behind a curtain, a voice was saying, "If you turn the volume all the way up but cut everything but the subwoofers, you won't hear a thing, but the hair on your arms stands up." We sat in a row of dentist chairs drinking beer from cans, talking quietly. "I don't want to drink too much," Lisa was saying to the man beside her. "I want to be awake for it." The host, busy arranging an aluminum operating table on wheels, evidently collected electrical equipment. Turning on the turbines ran his electric bill. He was saving them for a German art magazine that had promised to take photographs. Passing codeine around in beakers on a steel tray, milky, not entirely dissolved in the water, talking nervously, pouring beer over the residue in the bottoms of the beakers, swishing it around, gulping to replace them on the tray. Several small animals in glass bottles of formaldehyde sat on the toilet tank in the bathroom. "Bats," Brandon said. I would have gone back for a second look, but after the codeine had been passed around, there was a line outside the door.

Around midnight someone cranked up the music. "I want to be sober," Lisa said, making her way to the steel-wheeled operating table. I held her beer. We waited as the brand was heated with a blow torch. Pulling on my sleeve, she added, "But not too sober." I passed her sips from the can as she nodded. Three brands finished the job, the marks red and runny. Afterward she sat up on the table holding her beer herself, fielding questions about how it felt.

Greg, passing by at noon on the sidewalk, three days after I started the plant store job, stopped to say hello, mentioning he was having lunch with Trent on the other side of the market. An hour later Trent, in a tie, came into the shop, to ask for me at the counter. "Greg said you worked here," he said. "I expected to come in and find you all covered in dirt."

"I don't do the plants so much. Mostly the computer."

He splayed his hands on the counter, folding them together. "Aren't you going to show me around?"

I led him through the aisles. "So where do you keep the flowers?" he asked.

"No flowers," I said. "It's mostly seeds and hardware stuff." It was hot in the back of the store. He rolled his sleeves, giving a little shrug before walking out into the sun. Ten minutes later, passing through the shop's door again, he stepped to the counter, passing me a red rose wrapped in cellophane.

"See you around," he said.

PUBLISHED

I might have stayed on at the newspaper once the internship ended. Two editors asked if I wasn't planning to be back after sailing. But it hadn't crossed my mind to ask if I could, or to ask for a salary, and Mark said I needed a paying job.

They published a few of my stories. When the first one came out, to celebrate, I wanted a dinner party, waiting for my birthday to have a proper excuse. None of my friends had seen Mark's apartment. It would be a house-warming party. I left flyers in the newspaper's mailroom. Everyone from the old apartment would be there. And Todd's brother's boyfriend and Todd's brother. A colleague of Mark's and the colleague's wife. Mark didn't suggest inviting anyone from the sailing trip.

I'd never had a dinner party with a real dining table, a full set of china, and chairs. I spent the day planning to make plans, then deciding to relax, leaving the newspaper ostentatiously open on the dining room table. A pleasant day seemed the best way to get ready. And there was a last hit left in a box in my room. I was celebrating. Outside, it was sunny. I watched the highway from the rose garden, bees buzzing, the highway drifting in the distance, sound and sight, leaving nothing between my bench and the mountains across the bay but air and light, the roar of distant, more distant, traffic.

Setting the table, there were odd glints of light on the plates laying them out, which didn't seem normal. We'd never used the "good china." Their glint didn't seem natural. I laid napkins. Forks, knives and spoons. Turning a page of the newspaper—it seemed ostentatious between the plates—I laid it on the coffee table, and thought of dusting. There didn't seem to be anything to dust. I laid out glasses. Mark had set out some bottles of wine. It seemed ridiculous to set a dinner table at four in the afternoon. My watch read six. Going out to pick some roses, the quiet of the stairwell frightened me back. There was the issue of food. There were breadsticks. It was six-thirty.

I picked up the phone, punched some numbers, and, like an ungodly lucky sign, heard Lisa's voice.

"Happy birthday."

"What do you do when you're making dinner and there isn't any?"

"Well, you go to the store and buy food." Blocks away, yet in my ear in the room, her voice might have been coming from Antarctica.

"Don't say. I don't think I could *manage*, or know what to *do* there, if I could find it. This store."

Lisa found it perfectly normal that someone having an eight o'clock dinner party would go shopping for food at seven, and might want someone else along. It was a miracle of understanding.

"But what do you *cook* for ten people?"

"Pasta."

"Is it normal to serve it at a dinner party, this pasta of which you speak?"

"I'll be there in a minute. Give me twenty."

I sat on a couch. She'd be signaled by the doorbell. It seemed an odd way to mark her coming—an electric wire running through the building, shooting currents back and forth, up and down, for longer than any of us had been here, with no notion of us except as intervals between moments we pressed or waited for a button three floors below. Surely I hadn't just called someone to help buy pasta. Surely I'd imagined the whole dinner party. Mark would be home, and I'd be sitting on the couch beside a table set for ten. The bell rang, sounding nothing like Lisa. But that was the signal.

Making our way up the hill, into the florescent lights of the store, there were different kinds of pasta.

"The thinner the pasta, the faster it cooks," she said. So it was capellini.

"But sauce?" I asked, aghast.

"There's sauce."

"They have sauce? Isn't canned sauce . . . not really for dinner parties?"

"This one's not bad. How about some olives and bread. Maybe a salad?"

I walked down a yellow brick road with a magician. These and other things appeared in our cart, as if dropped from heaven. For money, there was a cashier to take it from me. That was the easy part.

Home, the pot boiling, its bubbles made a sheen on the water's surface, which for a moment I wanted to lick, then to spoon off and put in the trash. Mark came in with flowers, smiled at us, and went to pull off his suit.

The bell rang, anonymous. Brandon and Todd's brother and the brother's boyfriend came in. Then Mark's colleagues, a friend of Lisa's. I was in an aquarium, strange fish swimming around me. The chairs filled. Lisa brought our dish to the table. Mine swam on my plate. "You *are*, aren't you?" Brandon said, elbowing my ribs. The bell rang. The editor stood stock straight in the living room, brown-suited, stiff, looking around, taking a seat at the table. A silence passed. Faces looked expectant. Todd's brother dropped his fork. Brandon smiled. I gazed at my plate. Voices rose. I couldn't find the slightest sense in what was being said. Dessert appeared from nowhere. I took some plates to the kitchen. Todd's brother's boyfriend stood washing glasses at the sink. Mark came up behind him. "You can't hold them by the stem of the glass, but by the bowl," Todd's brother's boyfriend said, smiling back at Mark. They flirted.

Clearing the table, we sprawled on couches. The colleagues and the editor left. Brandon was headed to another party. Todd's brother and his boyfriend left with Brandon. Lisa stretched on the couch. Mark found his bathrobe. I lay on the carpet. The bell rang. We almost didn't answer it.

There was a flurry in the foyer. There was blood. It had been a baseball bat, an open convertible of men. Three, four of them stood in the bathroom, washing off the blood. Mark called two taxis.

"I'm not getting in a taxi and going home," Lisa shouted. "I'm going with you to the hospital."

Downstairs, under a lush quiet of trees, the taxis waited. We followed the first. "I'm not getting in a taxi and going home," Lisa persisted. Mark somehow steered the driver to her apartment door and put her out. We continued up the hill.

Lisa stood in the soft glow of the hospital carport. "But you're here!" I said.

"Where did you think I'd be? I called another taxi as soon as I got in the door."

We sat in the waiting room, watching them in the hall, standing, sitting, lying in line. We stood, sat, waited with them.

Todd's brother came out with one side of his jaw

wired shut. He wanted to smoke a cigarette. We got an orange soda at the gas station next door. "I shouldn't be smoking," he said. "I just quit two weeks ago." I handed him a couple more cigarettes before his boyfriend's sister came to pick them up.

It was three in the morning. Mark chided me in the taxi home for giving Todd's brother cigarettes. We turned out the lights. We slept.

MONOPOLY

I went over to Lisa's new apartment to see if she was there. She came to the door in jockey underwear and a denim shirt I'd found on the railroad tracks the year before.

"Hey," I said. "Want to get stoned and play Scrabble?"

"Yeah," she said. "I was going to go get coffee at ten o'clock. That's weird you came by."

"Yeah," I said. Her landlord had been out in the hall putting a sign up, so I took a towel and lay it along the crack below the door. I handed her the new Douglas Coupland book. She flipped through it, looking at the pictures over its chapter headings. She had this crazy new chair—a Louis XV thing with pink upholstery. She'd found it in the trash. Hair piled in coils on her head, she sat back with legs any model would kill for propped on the windowsill, all her tattoos on display. After a while, without putting the book down, holding it in one hand, then the other, she pulled on a skirt, and then another shirt. "So do you really want to get stoned and play Scrabble?" I said.

"Yeah," she said, not looking up from the book. "But don't they have Monopoly at Puss-Puss?"

"I don't know," I said.

"I think they do," she said.

"Okay," I said, "Let's play Monopoly then. Want to smoke some pot?"

"Do you *have* some pot?"

"Coffee's on me."

"Bottom drawer." She was still looking at the book. "We need to though," she said, "try to open that window."

"Okay," I said. "I'll tell you what I decided on my birthday."

"Okay," she said. She held her breath as if she'd inhaled the pipe with me, pointing to the window, miming blowing out through it.

"I didn't want to blow it out the window in case the landlord was out there."

"Why would the landlord be standing outside the window?"

"Maybe he was emptying the trash?"

"That's random." She looked up from the book. "So this birthday decision?"

"This birthday trip," I said, "Made my lips tingle. I went downstairs and got my birthday package from the landlady and went outside and opened it, which was really meaningful and everything. Then I went upstairs. I couldn't sit still, so I tried to meditate for a while, but couldn't, so wrote for a while, then stopped and worked on my résumé. There were shadows where the light didn't hit, moving shadows, in the corners. I went to the bathroom and the towels on the towel rack were waving back and forth."

"Weird," she said.

"Yeah. There was the brickwork on the building across the street, the sun hitting it. I wrote a story about a village that has a celebration, and the next year they decide to do it again. But the year before was so good they're afraid it won't be as good again. They plan a better party, with more food. It pops. So they want it better the next year. They get a bigger fire and servers and better food and more games. And every year they make it better and better. After a thousand years, with millions of servants to run the thing, the whole party is built on a huge mountain of ruins of all the castles and palaces where it was held before. Like that painting of the Tower of Babel you like."

Lisa thought for a minute. "Bruegel."

"Then I thought how birthdays are just celebrations of your ego. Like Imelda Marcos. Then I freaked out. So it wasn't that great."

"Any epiphanies?" she asked.

"That smoking is terrible."

"Well, you won't let *that* stop you."

"Nope. Did you hear about REM?" We had tickets. Brandon had called to say the drummer had a brain aneurism in Switzerland.

"I called my sister and she said MTV," Lisa said, "which,

sad as that sounds, is probably the definitive source at this point, said it was a very slight brain hemorrhage, and that he would be okay in a few days." Lisa was earnest about REM. She'd once had a soul-searching conversation with Michael Stipe in a bar in Athens, Georgia.

"A slight brain hemorrhage?"

"Yes."

"Maybe he just had a headache."

"Maybe," she said, pulling her boots on with one hand, the book in the other. "I think it was like just a capillary burst. They've never flaked before. I don't see why they'd flake out now. As far as I know, they're still playing. They don't have to operate. They just want him to rest."

"Todd's mom had an aneurism. She smoked so long her blood vessels popped. He said she used to sit on a couch and smoke and fall asleep. The arms of the couch were all covered with burns. He watched her once fall asleep and burn the couch."

"He didn't try to stop her?"

"I guess he didn't really think about trying to stop her."

"That refrigerator is really gross," she called, sinking into her chair with the book. "You really should close it before it starts to stink up the room."

"I got really thirsty all of a sudden," I said.

"Fancy that. Well, let's go get some coffee." She got up, pulling on my jacket.

We went out in the hall. A note from the landlord said the water would be turned off two days later that week. She moaned.

"They'll do it while you're at work," I said. "They wouldn't do it in the morning."

"With my luck I won't go to work, the morning they do it."

"Yeah. You might have a very slight brain hemorrhage and have to go in late."

We walked my bike to the corner of Pine, starting up the hill. At a phone booth, an old man in a ratty coat had an excited look on his face and held the receiver saying, *Yeah. I'm up on Capitol Hill tonight . . .*

The cafe had Monopoly, Scrabble, Life and chess. Our table was next to another couple who looked like they were on a first date. The boy was occasionally very intense with the girl, leaning forward, making his eyes shine as he spoke. The girl was reading, and kept looking up at him every now and then to see if he was still watching her. He usually wasn't, but she prepared a smile each time just before she looked up, anyway.

Lisa got a cookie, two coffees and a copy of some newspaper she thought was funny. I had the board set up but she wouldn't put down the paper. I rolled, moved and landed on INCOME TAX: PAY $200 OR 10%. I paid $200.

"Lisa, it's your turn," I said. She wouldn't look up from her paper. "Lisa . . ." We played. Putting down the paper, she paid attention, but I bought and mortgaged and put up houses. Every time she went around she paid me money, even though I was in jail a lot.

Outside, I pulled my Walkman on. She pulled my jacket collar up around her ears and said to be careful listening to music and biking. I hugged her. "Okay," I said, riding off, the volume turned up to speed down Bellevue.

RUMORS

Stories circulated about Trent that summer.

Greg and Trent were always slandering each other good-naturedly when the other wasn't around. Trent's jokes about Greg seemed more self-defense than anything else, but one afternoon, and for the rest of the summer, Greg's criticism seemed more pointed. Sometimes Mark was there when Greg told the latest dish on Trent, but I always felt it was told for my benefit. Most of the stories Greg told, I often got the idea Greg made a lot of the stuff up. Which wasn't wrong of him, really. Greg had an interest in keeping us apart since, in a way, he had brought us together. That summer I heard Trent had run up fifty dollars of phone sex on the line in Greg's boat. Trent had spent all his money on a weekend trip and had to call his parents to bail him out. Trent had almost lost his job again. He didn't return phone calls. I heard he never went out anymore, that he was always out every night of the week, that someone had seen him on Broadway drinking alone, with someone we didn't know, with a book.

We were supposed to take the boat out again with Greg. What started out as a clear day turned windy.

There was a small craft warning. Trent canceled, so Mark, Greg and I drove to Ray's Boathouse to sit on the deck. When it was bad weather at Ray's they brought blankets out to the deck. The sky was yellow-brown, the water choppy. A man in a wood dingy was out trying to get to the dock, but the tide kept pulling him back out. The wind kept knocking his boat against the piers. He balanced, a few feet from the dock, unable to reach it. We watched him, the sun low on the horizon, though you couldn't have said where it was, with the fog.

I had coffee. Mark and Greg had beer and pie, exchanging odd glances. I left the table to walk around the marina.

When I came back, they were talking about Trenton.

As they spoke, I heard Trent had gone to a party with someone, giving him cab fare on the front steps to send him home. Trent was dating someone with my own name, Ian, Ian Blanchman. Everyone approved of Ian Blanchman, said Mark, who approved of Ian Blanchman most, recounting where he was from and the software company he worked for and where he lived. He'd met Trent at Neighbors, on one of the supposedly rare occasions Trent frequented Neighbors.

On sailing trips, Trent supposedly moped, leaving early. I sat, trying to look disinterested. But I was lenient toward his shortcomings, even forgiving his drunken quotations, mangled plagarizations from back issues of

Vanity Fair. Trent had come out here, where family names meant little, for adventure, for something to give him his edge back. You can want something all the more for not wanting it completely. Or convince yourself you want it to the point of pain, hiding the fact you don't want it at all.

Trent had a party on the fourth of July. His houseboat was docked on Lake Union. Everyone had climbed through a skylight onto the roof to watch the fireworks over the lake by the time Mark and I rang the bell. He climbed down to let us in. If Ian Blanchman, the boy Trenton was supposedly dating, was among the dozen others on the roof among us, I tried not to discover. We followed Trent up the ladder through the skylight. Looking at his eyes, afraid I wouldn't stop, I looked at the far side of the lake, lowering myself along the slope of the roof, crouched to a position where I couldn't see his face. This is crazy, I thought, climbing down, opening the medicine cabinet in the bathroom, finding his cologne, smelling, noting its brand so as to get myself a bottle, stepping outside, walking to the end of the dock to watch the last of the fireworks alone.

Walking off the houseboat landing to the car, I tried to say something to Mark to encapsulate the thing happening to me, to find a story to make sense of it.

"You think I don't see?" Mark said, spitting at the

dashboard, turning to me. "Do you think everyone doesn't see?" He spat again at the steering wheel. "I'm not having this conversation."

Lying when reality hadn't corresponded to the things I'd imagined was a habit Isaac had pulled me out of. Now I was a good liar, trying not to, unsure reality and imagination could ever coincide.

Mark bought a computer for the apartment. Internet worked. Lisa emailed recipes.

Quick 'N Easy Recipe #24
Pork alla Don't Ask, Don't Tell

Rub skin of one small live hog with finely-diced fresh mint, molasses, tomato paste.

Collect children aged 6 to 13, feeding them as much candy as they can eat. Hand out butcher knives.

Release pig from kitchen into the back yard or street.

Tell the kids the first one to spear the pig gets his own Stealth Bomber.

Quick 'N Easy Recipe #25
SpaghettiOs alla Fornese

1 can SpaghettiOs

1 can Pork 'n Beans

1 box Cherry Jell-O

1 tbsp. chopped, salted liver

1 head Iceberg Lettuce

3 red grapes

2 tbsp. capers

Cool Whip topping, to taste

A quick shot of Final Net Hairspray

For this recipe you will also need:

    Wooden Spoon

    Chainsaw

    Medium-sized serving dish, warmed

SpaghettiOs alla Fornese can also be made "au flambé" by using more hairspray and a lighter. For a multicultural crowd, this recipe also doubles as "SpaghettiOs Allah Fornese." When entertaining the Religious Right, refer to it as "SpaghettiOs alla Jesus."

This all-purpose dish always goes well with big glasses of room-temperature pepper vodka.

In winter, an appetizer can be made from: 1 part Pork 'n Bean juice, 1 part gin, and 1 part peppermint Schnapps.

Quick 'N Easy Recipe #26
Chicken alla Gulf War

Clear a 4-foot radius with a small wire pen.

Place inside enough live chickens to meet the needs of your celebration.

Gather guests. Douse chickens with 2 parts Captain Morgan's Spiced Rum, 1 part gasoline.

Light. Serve hot.

Quick 'N Easy Recipe #27
Brownies à la Campaign '92

Mix hash, 2 cups milk, 1 cup sugar and 1 package of brownie mix.

Cook for 1½ hour at 150 degrees. Cool, serve.

Remind your guests to be sure not to swallow.

Quick 'N Easy Recipe #28
Meat Lover's Milkshake

1 cup milk

1 cup ice

3 frozen hot dogs

1 cup sugar

2 cups chocolate chips

Place ingredients in blender. Mix on high until foamy.

This simple recipe makes a refreshing protein-filled treat my family has enjoyed for generations.

Losing My Religion

Trent's cap still hung on the coat rack. I'd left it there after the sailing trip.

"Whose hat is this?" Mark asked one afternoon, packing for Alaska, though he must have seen it a dozen times before, hanging there.

"Trent's," I said.

"He doesn't like being called 'Trent,'" Mark said, folding his jacket. "His name is Trenton. 'Trent' is what his friends from the racing club call him, and he's too shy to protest. You should call him Trenton." His face reflected on whether to suggest returning the hat. Struggling to close his thoughts, closing his suitcase, propriety won over: "And you should give it back."

Easier done than said, Trent called half an hour after Mark left for the airport.

We met at the door of some club with a reputation he thought would be appealing to me and flattering to him, but which ended up being closed. We walked in the warm night through deserted South Lake Union. Buildings, fences, vacant lots ghosted at our sides, reeling, amorphous, dark ghosts as we moved, my attention only attuned to the nearness or distance of his arm, hand, leg to mine, measured in their warmth as they passed or glanced my own. There were no familiar landmarks. "This'll be a park some day," he purred, pointing left, but all I registered was his sleeve's proximity to my shoulder, the slight rise and fall of temperature in my elbow, depending on infinitesimal gradations of distance between us. An hour had passed when I looked at my watch. We were standing below Mark's building.

"I know the building," he said as we climbed the hill. "I lived here, the first year, when I first moved here." I flipped a switch, lighting the carpet. We climbed the stairs. "You can tell I'm from the East Coast from the way I lace my boots," he was saying, kneeling to unlace them, but all I saw was the outline of his ankle, his fingers.

"What's your religion?" he asked.

I opened the window, stretching on the rug beside him. "I figured it out this winter," I said. "When Carl Sagan died." Channel 4 had run a video clip from *Cosmos*.

Cosmos was the kind of thing my parents watched after I was supposed to be in bed. So I might have caught the first half of it, the opening credits. Sagan was something like John Denver, if John Denver wasn't blond, and talked about carbon atoms instead of singing. He came out onto the screen to explain mountains, rivers, and all the amazing breathless scenery of the earth, as Bach poured from the TV like the slow unfolding voice of God. As he looked around, smiling at the world as the music climaxed, you realized the universe, whatever it was, worked with the fixed pitch of the synthesized Bach playing in the background, and knew everything around us really is a great machine, still wound and ticking admirably, in misunderstood but knowable ways.

In one of the ways television still felt resonantly eerie in the days before internet, it'd triggered something I'd forgotten. A three-year old staying up past bedtime after being tucked in, sneaking into the living room. The glowing screen as the show starts from behind the couch, music already droning its synthesized passacaglias. An initiation of sorts—television after dinner. It wasn't that I thought of Sagan, coming out with his smile to explain the universe to his congregation of PBS viewers, as religion. Religion was Sunday school, a pocket-sized black New Testament, pages marked with my own ball-point-scrawled name that marked and claimed it. But the show had provoked something like a mystical experience. That I have a record of this now, online, accessible any time, is the wonder of our age, holy as the walls of the Lascaux caverns. *Behold, I bring you good tidings of great joy*, Sagan might as well have said to me and the rest of his three-year old audience. And, lo, though we walked through the shadow of the ensuing decade of *Dallas* and *Alf*, there appeared the promised land of DVDs, 150-channel cable and internet. Years later, when my father bought a telescope, we'd stood in the back yard watching the stars.

"And heaven?" Trent asked, fiddling with his socks.

A large, damp, foggy place, inside a cloud, like the clouds outside airplane windows, you wandered wet, foggy gold streets looking for relatives, searching for familiar faces in crowds of angels. Tall, dark, unfamiliar with their inhuman wings, close in a crowd, a disorganized receiving line. Later, someone told me the gold streets might have been something just made up, but the mansions were for sure. Quiet, like around Richmond Beach or Magnolia when a fog rolls in, with those big houses perched on their bluffs. As a child, the idea struck me that instead of wandering through crowds of dead people on cloudy gold streets, you might simply look up the addresses of dead relatives. Maybe they would even already know everything about you, telling it to you better than you knew it yourself. They might, in their mansions, make something for dinner, not food, but whatever angels drink. They'd be dead, and of course they'd be rationing casseroles and drinks for eternity—every glass of god-nectar they served would mean breaking into a store of good deeds done, for every time they'd emptied the trash, walked the family dog, or were nice to their sister at dinner in 1830, in 1930 or 1730 or 1230 or 30 or 3000 BC, as waves of grandchildren arrived at their doors, aglow with fresh faces of the newly dead.

"If you're around clouds all the time, then you can fly," Trent said.

Then I saw there might be no need for wandering between balustrades and gilded conservatories of banshee aunts and corpse-faced uncles when you might have your own pile on a hill above the smoggy angelic masses. Stained glass, and for every good thing you did, another panel of glass. There'd be no way to fill in the missing panes once dead, but while alive, you could try to finish it. Missing panes in your front door, bare patches in the parquetry would be annoying in Heaven, living with them for eternity. God might visit, or you might want to throw a party. A good deed might be worth a long row of cherubic friezes in a wing of rotundae, stretching out into cool boxwood paths. Good deeds might excavate a sunken rose garden, slip a grotto beneath the stairs. Or an afternoon of good works accumulate a chandelier's single crystal prism, a marble Apollo, a wall-sized Warhol, or move the pool west, making way for an orangery. Missionaries all over the world were converting people so fast that Heaven's gates were probably going to be like the lines on Ellis Island by the time you got there. I'd been converted in a garage by an over-zealous neighbor not much older than myself, whose parents had been missionaries. Her mother had a crafts desk in the garage. She'd handed me a block of pink pastel drawing chalk after we'd prayed, so the whole experience had seemed shady. Asking Christ into your life in a garage might be buying a mansion from the mafia. The second time I converted, I felt safer. I'd saved the mansion from my first time for my sister, in case she needed one once she was dead. She'd be safe, no reason to complain, as long as I kept up my good deeds.

"Can we go lie down for a while?" Trent asked, chin pointed to the spare room where I wrote, and sometimes slept, when Mark was out of town.

"Yeah, there's a futon."

"This is where you work?" We lay down. Trent leaned his head against the wall.

"I wish we were back on that island, lying on the grass with those deer," he said.

"Can I tell you a secret?" he asked.

I didn't answer. He was quiet for a while.

"Ian Blanchman is HIV positive."

"He told you?"

"Yeah."

I sat up to look at him. His eyes were expressionless.

"Oh, man, I'm sorry."

"It sucks. Like that thing you wrote." He looked at me. A review of Paul Monette the newspaper published that week. "He's, like, twenty-five. And so much energy. Like he has to go out and do everything, now, before he's thirty," he said. "Like he has to do it all so fast." I let him go on, his body cool and damp.

His mouth so cool, it wasn't kisses, but sharing breath, the same air.

Handing him his cap, a breeze rose from the Sound through the window, breaking the evening's heat.

Quick 'N Easy Recipe #29
Cow Ka Bob

Using a badminton post, one end filed sharp, skew one mature live cow, penetrating the anus, plunging the badminton net post firmly through the body till it comes out through the mouth. This process may take up to an hour. Be sure to plan the rest of the meal accordingly.

Cut off the legs (in the interest of the safety of our fellow picnickers, we sometimes complete this step first, depending on the age and energy level of the cow).

Roast over a large fire on the pole, turning frequently.

Slice meat directly from the body as it cooks.

Discard intestines and other internal organs, as the badminton pole usually ulcerates them and leaves them mushy.

Note:

For this recipe it's best to prepare the fire about an hour before cooking time, in order to have the coals hot enough. Hardcover books make the best kindling. The Pope has a complete list of books that work best, which you can obtain from your local bishop.

Quick 'N Easy Recipe #30
Magic Cucumbers with Slow Internal Bleeding Sauce

For those hot summer afternoons where the last thing you feel like doing is standing in a hot kitchen, but are unemployed and have sublet your bedroom, try this Quick 'N Easy surprise.

1 tsp. Battery Acid

1 tsp. Peppermint Oil

1 tsp. fiberglass insulation

Cucumbers

Watercress, washed and diced fine

Basil

Chop the basil and watercress. Mix with oil, acid and fiberglass.

Pour over diced cucumber.

For more rapid hemorrhaging, use more fiberglass.

For slower bleeds, serve on toast.

This meant she wanted to be asked out. She called from Café Paradiso to say, "Hey, what time do you want to leave?" the stagy edge in her voice letting me know she'd decided beforehand to say "what time" instead of "do you still want to go?" She knew I wanted to stay home, which made it impossible to say so. She was at the cafe's pay phone, straining to hear me over the music, people waiting behind her, and had probably already called everyone else she knew. I said about nine, then got on my bike and went over to her place. She was on the phone when I came in. "There's water in the refrigerator," she whispered, a hand clamped to the receiver. "Avoid the things in aluminum foil."

I pulled open the refrigerator door. "I didn't know mold could grow on aluminum."

"No way," she said, putting down the phone, coming to look.

"What was this?"

"Just some sort of pseudo-teriyaki."

We took our bikes down the hill together, mindful of each other in the dark on the steep hill like two people on a first date, calling out every block to see the other was okay, taking the final hill in one fast swoop together with a mutual thrill as the freeway rushed and thundered below our tires. The bar had live garage with dollar beers. It was nearly dead except for an eight-seater booth full of what appeared to be immediate groupies and seedy yet expensive-looking guys with mustaches. There was an old man in a hat dancing wildly without music, who might have been an eccentric regular except that the security was eyeing him suspiciously.

The guy next to us was saying, "So I spent half the summer in the Midwest and everyone there was like, oh my god, what is up with your hair, it's so weird. So I didn't meet any cute guys, but I met these three totally cute girls—" We never heard the end of his story because on that word the band took the stage, struck out a drum beat, and a trumpet wailed into the microphone. The room was dark and we danced, wildly but half-heartedly. A row of muscle-bound surfers swayed in the background, urged on by their seventeen-year-old girlfriends until, sweating, they pulled off their shirts to slam-dance, for lack of any better way to show their appreciation for the band. We drank because the drinks were only a dollar after the cover charge, and because neither of us wanted to go home.

"I'm thinking about getting rid of my dreads," Lisa said. We leaned against a pillar sweating. "This girl who works at Rudy's convinced me I could actually get the locks out without cutting them." The band wailed. "With the right products."

"Brandon might not recognize you."

"Fuck Brandon. He's probably got his dick up some someone's ass right now." Dollar beers get expensive when they're served in tiny cups and you're sweating, but we were both pretty drunk.

"At least with dread locks you never really have good hair days and you never have bad hair days. Every day is more or less just a day."

"It's Prozac for hair." The next band had a squealing speaker. I had to shout to be heard. "You can do it, Lisa, break free."

"I'm just not sure I'm ready to start having bad hair days again. I seem to remember having a lot of them before."

"There's probably been all kinds of innovations in hair care products since then."

"Like you'd know, Mr. Chloral Herbal Essence. You've had the same haircut since the day we met."

"Which isn't that long," I shouted.

"For this city it's a long fucking time, Ian," she shouted. A band with a bad speaker decided to start anyway, and we lost each other as the slam-dancers found their second wind.

Inversion

Mark's case kept him in Anchorage. The weather was stinking hot that week.

Brandon called that weekend. "We're all going out Thursday with Ian, that guy Trent's dating. Trent's in charge of picking a movie, and he'll pick something horrible. He'll be at your place early. I'll come by to pick you up. I'll be late." The weather was broiling.

Ian Blanchman rang the bell first, a smile glimmering in the doorway. He had a healthy Midwestern neck, thick as the sides of his head, shaking my hand as Trent came up the stairs behind him. I offered them beer. Ian Blanchman, scanning refrigerator options, took juice. Trent took a position a corner. Ian Blanchman moved up to him, was ignored twice, and took the other side of the room, nursing his juice on the arm of a couch.

"Play the piano," Trent said.

"It's a silly old synthesizer," I said, "I hate to."

Brandon rang downstairs as the sun went down. "I didn't know they were coming *together*," he whispered in the kitchen, looking over his shoulder into the living room.

The week's windless heat had packed itself on so there was barely room to breathe in the apartment. I drank half a beer, passing it to Trent to finish. We hung by the living room windows until it was obvious no breeze was coming up from the bay, even after sunset, then took off for the Harvard Exit.

"It's an inversion," Brandon said. We mounted the hill toward the Cornish Café, sweating through our shirts. "The sun and moon are in conjunction, and the clouds are pressed between them," Brandon was saying. We shot glances down the hill toward the finished sunset. The moon lay on the horizon, thick and hazy at a distance. Trent and Ian Blanchman walked behind for a while, till Trent fell a block behind us, calling up huskily, "Brandon! Call a cab! These hills are killing me!" Brandon and Ian Blanchman laughed. I stood outside the theater, watching Trent climb the sidewalk alone.

His breath hit my cheek as he came up the steps, a shoulder brushing mine, a long, slow brush sending me toward the door jamb. He laughed, shoving me into the lobby. The curtains pulled apart, the sun set, velvet pulled open to show the lit street and the red haze over the bay. It was air-conditioned. It smelled like floor wax, brass polish, mildewed velvet. I saw none of the film. Halfway through it, I realized that moment at the door was all I'd thought about since it began.

They were going on to Broadway to drink afterward. I left them on the sidewalk with an unconvincing excuse, red-faced as they walked off.

Hot blasts wafted from the Sound, passing through the strip of overpasses around Lake Union, and smelled it. Red clouds poured into the air above downtown's scattered glowing skyscrapers. The skyline pulsed, sparkling, nodding toward the void at its western edge, the water in its pitch black bay. I descended the hill. From the park behind the building, the moon rose higher, huge and brick red, swelling through the clouds, then shrinking to take its final steps toward the sky's center. My watch said I'd been sitting there an hour.

Inside, a red halo on the black bay glared on the windows facing ours across the street. The ceiling, the bed sheets had a reddish cast, a nebulous neon glow. Lightning flashed. The room shook. *Ian's inversion is over*, I thought, going back to sleep. The buzzer rang downstairs. Rain was slapping at the windows.

"...Me," said his voice in the intercom.

I pulled the door open. At the top of the stairs, his hands plunged into his pockets, his pants leaked from their cuffs on the carpet, hair plastered wet to his forehead. I handed him a towel. He stalked past me to the living room, his head in his hands. "I couldn't get a taxi," he said hoarsely, looking up to catch my eye. "Was the movie awful?"

"I didn't watch it."

"Me neither. I'll sleep on the couch."

I brought a blanket, laying it over him.

"I won't sleep if you're out here," I said.

"You won't sleep if I'm in there with you," he said.

We went to the bedroom and lay there for five or six hours. Lightning flashed red on the ceiling. I kept falling asleep, forcing myself awake to hear his breathing.

As a child, waking up in hotels, I'd lie for a minute, eyes closed, lost, trying to visualize where I was before opening them to see. That morning was like that. At some point he must have gotten up to close the blinds. The room was dark. I had no idea where, when, or who I was. I knew nothing except that he was there breathing beside me, and that the room was cooler now. Slowly, I placed the bed. The day. The city. The room. We must have slept apart. But now it was morning. I had to get to work. We found each other's arms till the alarm clock went off. Outside the window, the sidewalk was dark with rain.

I boiled water. Poured in oatmeal. He shuffled bottles in the medicine cabinet for aspirin, tossing a cigarette out the window with a smile, coming up behind me at the stove, an inch away, the warmth from his chest radiating on my back.

"Is that what starving artists eat for breakfast these days?" he asked, touching his nose to the back of my neck.

"This is it. Raisins inspire the muse."

He'd moved to the window, disappearing as I turned back to the kitchen to finish breakfast, closing the front door behind him without a sound.

I called Mark from work that afternoon.

"Well, hello," he said, a mix of condescension and curiosity in his voice.

"Hi," I said.

"Have fun last night?" Mark asked.

"It was all right."

"Mmm *Hmm*."

RENT

I didn't want to go out. Mark had connected his computer to the internet and I wanted to stay home making Italian food, writing. I imagined I wrote better when I was online, hooked up so that each line was sent off immediately, without revisions, no changes—this was it—everything perfect now, even if I was only sending it in a message to myself. But I'd told Lisa I'd go to the Off Ramp to hear some bands play, and it was three dollars, so I had no excuse.

She'd left a reminder in an email that afternoon, with recipes from her book of office terrorism:

Computer Crafts
Project 1: Floppy Disk Hula Dancer

The perfect gift to leave as a surprise "Thank You!" to a special co-worker on the day you quit or your project is terminated.

It's simple, fun, easy-to-make, and takes just minutes to complete.

You will need:

    2 or 3 floppy disks

1 pencil

An exacto knife or scissors

Roller ball from a mouse

2 sticks freshly-chewed gum

Cut the casing from the disks, removing the interior floppy disks.

Using the scissors or exacto knife, make a series of straight cuts from the inside outward about ¼ inch apart.

Remove the roller ball from your mouse. Drawing a happy face on one side of it with the pencil, attach the roller ball to the eraser side of the pencil with (chewed) gum, shoving the point of the pencil through the floppy disks' centers.

Now you have a Floppy Disk Hula Dancer.

Stick the (chewed) gum to the point of the pencil, attaching the entire project to the desk surface.

For an extra special touch:

Shove the point of the pencil into the disk drive of the owner's computer. In this case you will want to attach the hula dancer's head so that she is smiling out toward the viewer.

Make appropriate arrangements to leave the building with your personal belongings before your gift is received.

I'd looked at my bank account, and I realized I had enough money to see a dentist. Meeting Mark for dinner afterward, I could only taste on one side of my mouth. Unable to tell if the coffee was hot or cold, I sat watching him eat. We went to a bar for glasses of Chianti. He got me a straw. He was back from New York, with the soundtracks from *Rent* and *Chicago*. *Rent* was supposed to be all grunge music and he said it was about artists living in lofts, but it sounded like every other musical I'd ever listened to. He'd been reading Edmund White and while we were talking about writing and drinking our wine, he said something about writers getting too close to the source, or the soul, or the sun, or something, like Prometheus, and have to have their livers eaten out by cirrhosis. We tried to remember what we could about Greek medicine, and the different kinds of biles, and whether Greeks would have known what livers are for. We argued over splurging on a new translation of the *Odyssey* someone had done.

Greg showed up. The bar was packed. Mark and Greg could stare as much as they wanted and it was completely harmless in most cases, but if I stared at someone they thought I was cruising them and they came over close to where I was generally, and then it took about five minutes of strong body language to convince them I was actually with someone. So I spent my time being resentful that I couldn't look at anyone, like they could. The Harvard Exit was playing *Star Wars*. On the sidewalk, Greg was telling us how the Force was the most important part of the movie. There was something a little unconvincing about the way he talked, like he knew he was right, but like you could tell he didn't really feel anything about it, or at least, not in the way I did or Mark did, like he was reciting something he'd read in a magazine. As Greg talked, I looked at Mark for a second and saw him smirk in a patronizing way, but so slightly that Greg probably took it for a smile. Staring at Mark's lips, seeing it wasn't a real smile, I had a kind of shock. He'd never looked at me in that way, unless I did something really awful. His eyes narrowed. Looking back at Greg, I felt like I was listening to a second-grader recite some complex, beautiful poem in a mono-tone. It was obscene like that, the way he talked about the Force, like hearing a ten-year-old talk about sex.

I woke early in a foul mood to dress for work, clomp-ing around the apartment in my boots eating yoghurt, speaking conversations from an imaginary kids' TV show called Mr. Quimbletobble's Tree House, where Mr. Quimbletobble and young Skippy gang rape Skippy's mother. It didn't shock Mark. Maybe he wasn't listening.

STARBELLY

I never told Trent when Mark was going out of town. But often as not, he'd call that afternoon, to meet at a club he didn't feel comfortable going to alone, or having heard I was going somewhere, wanting to meet me there. We rarely went out, though. He would stop by and I'd sit listening to the sound of his voice asking about the book I was reading, keeping my answers as short as possible to hear him speak again. He'd stand by the window in my room, push the futon to the windowsill, letting our shoulders graze. We never hugged when he came to the door, but following me from place to place, he stayed close enough that I could feel the heat from his skin wherever he was in the room.

He pulled the window open to look out. "We were talking about Brandon last night," he said. "How he purses his lips when he doesn't like something. How he bikes and kayaks and runs and has this sense of himself."

"He doesn't see himself the way his friends do, you mean?"

"No." He thought for a minute. "But he'll probably outlive us all. He's so healthy."

"You'll have a heart attack at sixty-five—the way you eat and smoke. Mark will live to be eighty. I'll probably . . . I don't know . . . And Greg will drink himself to death by sixty. But Brandon . . . I don't know. He's healthy in some ways, but he's worse off than anyone in other things." I'd almost fallen asleep beside him.

"What do you mean?" he asked, squinting at me, that way that was the most incredible thing about him.

"I mean his kayaking and biking, his drugs, all the things he does. He doesn't do any of it for his health."

"Brandon likes pain, you mean," he said. "He can't leave it alone. People like that can't stay away from it. He keeps coming back to it. It's all he really likes about everything he does."

"Unlike you."

"Don't criticize me for coming here." He squinted. He stared at me. I was afraid if I looked at his eyes too long I wouldn't stop, so kept looking across the room at the window, then back again. "No, but he'll probably outlive us all."

One afternoon Mark had gotten home early and said he'd called while I'd been at Puss-Puss after work reading Holleran. Trent wanted to take me to a party. I told Mark, as casually as I could, that I'd go. "Good," he said. "Maybe you two should talk." Trent rang from downstairs at about eight-thirty and I went down.

"I'm confused," he said outside. "I don't know what I

want, and I don't know, if I do want it, if I should." Brandon pulled in front of the building and we drove around Fremont looking for the party. We couldn't find it, so we went to R and sat there with a pitcher, Trent glaring alternately at the table and at me, Brandon pretending to cruise other men at the adjoining tables. "They've broken up, Trent and Ian Blanchman," Brandon said, leaning in. I sat very still between them, the room swaying now with all its movements, noise and laughter, as Brandon finished the pitcher, too drunk to be of any use, and Trent slowly downed his glass, his glare intensifying as his fingers rubbed the gloss of the tabletop. On the sidewalk, his heels turned the corner, the air behind him visible, quavering, a nest of fresh autumn leaves swirled by the wind in their wake.

I walked down Broadway, Brandon shouting cheerfully at passing couples, and went home, strangely glowing.

Mark flew to Alaska. Trent called. We agreed to meet for coffee, or dinner, or something, and make an early evening of it. He came to the door in a department store copy of the T-shirt from R.E.M.'s tour. We went to Bailey Coy and looked at books. It was the end of a rainy day he'd spent watching Wimbledon and I'd spent crouched over a desk at work bringing UPC codes up on a computer screen. The sun was almost out. People on

Broadway were chipper. We talked about racism, gun control, and jackbooted thugs pulling themselves up by their bootstraps. Noticing my face blank, he pulled me into every store from the corner of John to Belmont. It was wet. We moved under the awnings, standing closer so the cold didn't blow between us, looking at things, seeing people, but all I registered was the heat between us, growing, dissipating as we moved closer or a little further apart. We reached the end of Broadway, the Cornish art school's miniature Mount Vernon, its gabled roofs, its air of rainy English village dropped in the center of Capitol Hill.

We went into a Safeway. He looked for dinner food. I got turkey slices, bread, cheese, and a tomato. He got crackers and salmon cream cheese spread. I pulled some cheese off the rack, leaving it on a display table. "You're not careful," he said, in the quiet, musing way people interested in a subject sometimes speak aloud, almost unconsciously, about their discoveries.

"When you left that last morning," I was saying. He held the umbrella over us. "You made me think people aren't as bad as I was beginning to think they were. I didn't want you to go, but I felt better about people than I had in a long time."

"I restored your faith in humanity?" he asked, raising an eyebrow with a smirk.

We climbed to the apartment. He sat on the rug with

his crackers, turning on the TV. I sat on the couch. He turned, giving me a funny look over his shoulder, which meant, "Why are you sitting on the couch?" So I sat down beside him, reaching my hand out, realizing I'd do anything, knowing I didn't care what we did anymore. If we could create a universe of gestures and looks communicating everything so clearly, it hardly mattered what else we did. We held each other in stints. He sat back, looking at the television as if it might after a time redraw his interest, then stood, moving to the door.

"I should call a cab," he said.

"Don't," I said. "Or do. Or don't. Don't you see nothing matters now?"

"No," he said, gazing at the room as if to memorize it as he held the phone. "This matters."

ATHENS ALEXANDRIA VIENNA
LONDON UNREAL
LONDON BELFAST AND BERLIN

I could have imagined everything else we could have said or done. But I was done imagining.

Monday, Mark announced he'd found a job on the other side of the country. Then very late, outside a club in Pioneer Square, Brandon was shot dead.

The funeral was in Alabama. Lisa didn't answer the phone that week. After a few phone calls, I realized no one I knew really knew Brandon, though his death was all anyone talked about when you saw anyone you knew.

Mark made arrangements for movers. He asked if I'd come with him.

We drove around the city, up Western, down Broadway, to the park, around the Lakeview Cemetery. The gym, the grocery store, and home. I made pasta and asparagus. Then I had a sip of cognac and a cookie and sat in the little room reading for two hours, smoked a cigarette, brushed my teeth, and laid on the futon in the spare room. I waited for a while. The light went out in the other room. I was a little surprised he didn't come in to make me come to bed, but just as I was on the very edge of sleep, he came into the room and asked if I was asleep. If he'd waited two more seconds I wouldn't have been able to answer him probably, but he crawled onto the futon beside me and said he couldn't sleep, and started to cry, and said he loved me, and I told him I loved him. The spare room didn't have an alarm clock, so we went into the bedroom and saw it was only six, but didn't want to oversleep, so we got in bed there. "Thanks for spending the morning with me," he said. I fell back asleep.

I went to a cafe on Broadway. I was hungry but I couldn't afford the food, so just drank an Americano and smoked. I didn't feel like doing either, which was stupid and kind of made me sick. I sat there for an hour or two doing both. It was one of those places where they play the radio over the speakers, and when the advertisements come on they just let them play, so a good quarter of the time you're trying to read or think, you hear over-excited voices talking about washing machines or cars or chewing gum. It didn't seem to bother anyone else.

Out with Greg that week, the conversation turned quickly, earnestly, to the question of what I would do for work in the city we were going to.

"They have Starbucks everywhere now," someone at our table was saying. "Coming from Seattle, he can always find a job as a barista."

But I wasn't going to stay.

Quick 'N Easy Recipe #31
Hard Liquor
(a traditional Hanes family favorite)

Drink it straight.

Sit, bored, for about 5 minutes while you wait for it to hit you.

Feel great for about 20 minutes. Wonder why you don't do this more often.

Pass out alone, in an uncomfortable position.

Wake up, crack a window.

Sit on the floor smoking a cigarette.

Credit card applications had been coming in the mail. All they asked about was household income. I'd filled them out honestly enough. The first platinum card came back with my name on it. I applied for three more. Outside the university bookstore, they handed them out like religious tracts. I half expected something to go wrong when I took the first card to a travel agency. But the receipt for a plane ticket came out of the travel agent's printer just the same as if I'd bought coffee or a newspaper.

I packed Mark's furniture, quietly getting rid of my own, reducing everything I owned until it fit into a single backpack. I went over to Lisa's with the plane ticket in my pocket. While Lisa lay on my lap sobbing, talking, and sobbing, I stared at the Trent Reznor poster over her bookcase, rubbing her arm. But when she stopped crying, lying inert across my knees, I saw it wasn't all about Brandon. She said she knew she was selfish to want me to stay, describing our lives separating, how we'd be years from now when we talked about each other to our friends. "You'll be just stories I'll tell friends who won't understand, and I'll be just a name you mention on some other continent to people who don't care."

We were listening to Brandon's REM CDs, drinking his Jägermeister, the last thing I'd saved. She stopped crying to ask how I was, sitting up. I'd spilled Jägermeister all over my pants and they were in the sink and I got up and sat in the chair by the window to tell her how I felt. And that was that I didn't know anything anymore, and felt sad, missing anything to believe in, but not really expecting to. From her eyes' glaze, I felt my words were kitsch, even as they rolled from my mouth. I couldn't twist any irony into anything I was saying. I wanted to go to Europe and sit on a cliff and think. She said I was much less crazy than when she first met me, and that if I wanted to go to Europe I should put on a suit and find a job and save money.

But I didn't see myself in a suit.

I traveled for a while, working as I found work, running up credit cards as I went. At first traveling itself seemed like a big deal. Once, twice, standing in line, glancing up from a book in a train station, seeing a head of black hair or the way someone stood, I felt an inner yelp of recognition. A face from a distance held something of his, then, drawing closer, always lacked something. I couldn't help hating them for it. The same mouth but not the same smile, the same shape of the eyes but a different forehead.

It's hard to hold on to something and to defend it at the same time. One arm drags the thing you love along, the other arm wrestling what stands in your way. At some point I dropped what I was holding, shoving with both hands. In the end, only moving forward seemed important. The traveler climbing a mountain in the direction of a star, if too absorbed by the logistics of the climb, risks forgetting which star guides him, moving only to move, going nowhere, says Antoine de Saint-Exupéry.

Sitting at a Vietnamese place, its waiter with one milk-white-eye, explaining the whole story to someone over a table, talking about Seattle, wondering how to end it, his suggestion was "something unexpected." Pacing a train platform, I hoped that as I finished the last chapters something would just come.

I found things to do wherever I went. Once I'd seen pretty much everything I'd ever wanted to see and done pretty much everything I'd ever wanted to do and run up enough debt that it took half of what I was making every month to pay for things I'd already seen and done—with an eerie shiver, leaving the restaurant, I'd realized Lisa's prediction had come true—I'd gotten a job, and even put on a suit. Then one day, I started thinking about Seattle again, and things seemed simpler every time I thought about it.

So one afternoon, years later, I found myself at Ray's Boathouse across a table from Mark, clinking ice as a martini breathed its first silvery whisper, on the verge of explaining, to a face changed in a dozen ways, each past length of explanation. The words nearly on my lips, I dropped my napkin on the table, heading out the doors, gazing over Ray's parking lot, then getting in a car, closing the door and driving home on an empty stomach, giddy with gin, memory, and, the mountains shining in the sun across the bay, a funny hope that, whatever evidence to the contrary, anything and everything was still possible on the New World's outer edge. That the past could be forgotten.

That's how I thought of things, that first month back. I'd tried to configure my thinking toward imagining a return to Seattle would be like a Fitzgeraldean character's return to the Midwest from Europe: a safe nest at the world's ragged edge. That didn't happen. My bus driver had a Georgian twang, my bank teller was Floridian. Midwesterners flocked through SeaTac each day, great belches of money throwing condominiums up like explosions. Downtown superstores' lights flashed like lighting. Malls swarmed with people from SUVs stacked six stories below floors of pressure-treated marble. The last decade's imports settled in hinterlands beyond the freeway. For the first time, Seattle seemed an American franchise.

Tourist shops on the islands didn't sell bottles of shells or cedar boxes anymore. They sold mouse pads with pictures of boats, leather wallets, and navigation software. But the marina's restaurant tables had the same contours, and the way Greg looked me in the eye frankly before asking the question I now saw he meant to ask from the beginning of this walk reminded me of seeing cousins every summer as a child: That period of staring at a stranger before you remember how to act and everything suddenly switches back as if you hadn't spent time apart.

From the marina's edge, they shouted to us through the morning fog, their voices disappearing instantly, lost in the space of the bay. "I've never been able to drink and walk at the same time," Greg was saying, so we took our coffee to a corner of the restaurant. We sat looking out at the bay. The reason he wanted to sit a while was to ask me this: "Everyone still wants to know," he said, his eyes turned down in shyness or a simulation of shyness, "Did you and Trenton really never . . . you know," smiling a confidential smile that promised anything but confidentiality, stressing *really* and *never* as if either might be something miraculous, astounding. The thing that might finally resolve me.

His eyes on me, I gazed out the window. The sun lifted the fog over the bay, lighting the table where we sat holding our coffees, warming our hands, and I could see he didn't quite believe me.

Lisa and her boyfriend live in a white clapboard house with a white picket fence. Every morning, the boyfriend gets up at ten o'clock, opens a cold can of frappuccino, goes into the living room and sits at the computer checking his stocks. At about ten-thirty Lisa goes in to stand behind his chair with her hands on his shoulders, giving a little massage, then waters the potted plants lining the big picture window. They're amazingly healthy plants, the light coming into the room all dark and luminous like stained glass in a green cathedral. The boyfriend hadn't been happy with the water pressure when he'd bought the house, so he re-tapped the water main. If you turn the shower all the way up, it pounds you like a masseuse.

Pettily, every time I looked at the boyfriend, it went rumbling through my head in circles: *Millionaire. Millionaire. Millionaire.* I got past the fact, but then there it was again. After a few days, you realize you tend to give millionaires more slack than you give people without a million dollars. He talks and you look at his eyes, then his eyebrow and the way his glasses fog as they push up against it after he's been jogging. Then you're like, *Oh, but he's a millionaire.* And then you start to wonder about yourself. I'd read that in America four people became new millionaires every day.

One sunny day while their kitten Tamaguchi was out being shampooed, Microsoft had gone up ten points and they were in a good mood. They were having juice and a bagel at the counter by the sink reading copies of *Wired*. I suggested a hike. Lisa's boyfriend pulled out about ten hiking guides, spreading them across the counter to have us look through them. Most of the really tall mountains still had snow on the trails, but one had a walk to a lake that was supposed to be clear, with a waterfall on the way up. The boyfriend filled some water bottles and went down to the garage to get the car. He was wearing shorts. For a retired person, he had really white legs.

Flowers bloomed along their driveway. As he backed down the drive, Lisa's boyfriend asked where we ought to stop for lunch supplies and when Lisa didn't say anything, he said, "Didn't you hear me?" When Lisa didn't say anything again, he said, "I asked you a question." The car lurched to a stop at the bottom of the driveway. A couple of zinnia heads nicked at the bumper, flying back on their stalks as if drunk.

"Oh, my goodness," Lisa said, sounding kind of scared because he'd said it so loud. "I'm sorry, my head is just pounding, I can hardly think." I'd never heard her say "oh my goodness" before, and wondered what she was really thinking of saying.

Her boyfriend said, "Well, if you have a headache why don't you take some ibuprofen," in a nicer voice. There was ibuprofen in the glove compartment, and they both took some. The boyfriend was talking about pollen. "It's amazing all the various things that can make your sinal tissues inflame," he said. "Pollen, or a change in the air, or mold, or sleeping the wrong way." It was cool, he said, that little twenty seconds or so when you can actually feel the ibuprofen start to work. *Zing!* he said. *Like that,* making a little wave-like motion with one hand while he drove to illustrate the zing, but Lisa said she never really felt it that way herself.

Off the main highway, sloping white barns sat in fields surrounded by new tract houses, the grilles of trucks for sale butting up against the side of the road with colored plastic flags. We stopped beside a low building with wood letters spelling out "Norm's TV" stuck on the roof, so we could pee at McDonald's after our coffee and soda. You could see the top of the moun-tain. The boyfriend said when the clouds hang around the middle of it like that, and not at the top, it means it's nice up there.

Crossing an iron bridge over a gorge, the boyfriend turned off the air conditioning and put the windows down. It smelled not so much like the trees, though that was there, too, but of something stronger and better. A flood of melting ice ran down from the glacier. You smelled fresh, ionized wafts of air from molecules being pounded apart on stone, the friction of cold water against the rocks and air. The trees layered in dark green bands with great horrible bare patches from logging along the ridge. I tried to breathe and breathe and focus on the smell of the air. A flood had washed a swath of gray stones across the road, which was blocked by a chain at the trailhead by the ranger's station. If we left the car in the ranger's lot, it was six miles to the falls, then another two to the lake, walking. Lisa hadn't worn socks. The boyfriend didn't say anything, but was annoyed.

"I should have brought a novel so I could just read while you guys go off climbing this . . . treacherous . . ." Lisa clumped through the creek bed that had been a road two weeks before ". . . mountain." Her raincoat was a hue of lime that exactly matched the colors of the new ferns along the trail, their tiny new tendrils curled into damp spirals at their ends. I unfurled a few, stroking the green hairs' tips with my finger. Having been taught as a child that ferns were very delicate garden plants that must never be touched, it was a singular, childish pleasure to stand in a waist-high forest of them, an awful shock to have the tips break off between your finger and thumb at the gentlest tug. When she walked in Seattle, Lisa said, the raincoat seemed almost violently bright. In the rainforest, it was nearly camouflage.

Lisa's boyfriend carried a tiny camera, moving around to take photos of Lisa. He took a picture of me to be nice, or maybe so Lisa could look at me on her computer later, if she felt like it. It was shady in the forest, but after a while the trail wound out of the shade into the sun, circling the peak where the lake was supposed to be. We would have driven this far if the road hadn't been out, we were all thinking now, Lisa probably most of all. The two of them took turns putting water on each others' necks. Up the trail we spread out, me ahead, waiting for them on bends as the path snaked up under the trees. Lisa looked happy, and wasn't hurrying to catch up. Sometimes her boyfriend took a picture of her as she walked, and she didn't pose or anything, but just kept walking and smiled.

Eventually you could hear the falls. The kind of white noise you only notice at first as an increasing absence of sound. Stronger came a scent that wasn't a smell, but a gradual absence of smell. A white smell, not conveying anything or telling you anything, just clearing other things away, leaving your thoughts naked. It was like you'd been thinking something, then realized the rhythm of your own thoughts, bobbing up regularly to the surface of a bath, and now the water was drained away, leaving them immobile, in whatever position they lay, at the bottom of the tub. Around that last bend in the trail before the falls, all your thoughts, even that last naked one, went blank in its presence.

The drop was thirty or forty feet, the smack of the water on the rocks below not so much water as energy dropped into the forest among the roots and ferns and branches. If people worshiped waterfalls, it wasn't because they said anything. They might have cured headaches or relaxed muscles or cured swollen feet, but the falls' voice didn't have any stories to tell. It blanked out everything else, an unpausing breath. Nothing grew at its very center where water smacked continuously on the rock below. Moss climbed the sides of the pool. A tree reached its lower branches toward the water, and down below a few branches, ripped off, lay in shreds, split wood spiked yellow, where the falls surged with melted glacier. On the edges, things thrived, greener, cleaner, growing faster at two feet from it than at four, at four feet more than forty. I moved away from the trail to wait, so Lisa and her boyfriend could take in the falls as they came up without seeing me, to discover it themselves.

The boyfriend came up the trail first, with an appreciative smile, a little hesitant, verifying the falls' height before giving them his full attention. Lisa came up. They held hands, glad when I came back down the trail and they could see me. The mist cooled you right down after the walk up, and we decided to climb on to the lake. Lisa was out of breath. Her boyfriend and I both hoped she made it to the top without saying anything unwhole-some. Tired, she could say things so scolding they made your heart ache. Things you knew, as she did, she already regretted saying, but sounding so reasonable, the way she said them, making them so much worse. We hung back, letting her take her time up the trail. The last bit was a stiff climb. Then we were there, on the shore of a lake with the pine trees and boulders. The boyfriend wiped the sweat mustache under his nose. Lisa smiled a lot. There wasn't a sound, not the slightest hum of insect.

They took pictures of birds they'd lured with biscotti crumbs. I left them to walk around the lake. A trail wound around the water, but petered out in some scruffy pines. I turned around. There was Wiccan crap between the rocks. Burned, probably thrown into the lake, you couldn't tell how long it had been there, but you could see they were careful Wiccans, reading from some instruction manual, probably, when they did the thing. Bringing their problems to a mountain. Making rocks that had sat quiet for thousands of years mark personal problems that probably resulted (it had to, with Wiccans) from their not being sure enough about something in the first place. Mountains don't come down to your house and make little marks on it when they have problems. Mountains don't give a damn. So you take your problems to them, and they say, in whatever nice way you want to hear it, "I don't give a shit." And you figure you should care a bit less yourself.

We went out to concerts a few times after I found my own place. Once, as we stood outside watching the pink dot of Mars rise, the band ending a set, she turned her head to me, finishing a long-ago conversation and said, "You have good hair days and bad hair days, Ian. You just have to appreciate the good ones when they come." On the steps beside us a man turned, speaking to two girls, but all we could hear of his conversation was, "So the West Coast, huh?" as the band began again, and with a whine of strings we were dancing.

I rented a studio, its deck sunk between two parking garages by the viaduct. Planting the deck with basil and ivy, I mailed rent to a programmer indefinitely retired to Mexico, once a month tracing an address I couldn't pronounce onto an envelope, sliding in a check for seven hundred dollars. I understood I was getting a deal. The building's other tenants, ball-capped middle-aged men, appeared from the islands on weekends to see women or crunch numbers. My view from the deck was of an oversized American flag strapped to the top of a glass elevator, spotlit evenings, lugging tourists from the parking lot to the market mornings, where they amused themselves watching aproned men throw frozen fish, browsing sales bins outside the anarchist bookstore. I sat watching the flag wave, listening to helicopters drone across the bay, carrying the rich or the dying, till the sun set, and Mars rose high above the viaduct.

Does distance between things eat the sound of your voice in Seattle? That summer I was convinced it wasn't distance, but the hushing roar of traffic, whose course must never be impeded. Everyone was complicit in this. Even on cell phones, people waited for traffic to pass before finishing conversations. Things must move. Entropy is our enemy, as we find ourselves propelled forever more distantly between locations that are homes, sites that are jobs, spaces that are love, tallied numbers showing the limits of what can and can't be had.

I saw Trent once more, too, that fall.

It was election season. The television had been spouting a series of bewildered nonsense in an endless loop since long before midnight at Greg's place, where, on the couch, we'd watched the first returns. After the polls closed, I'd gone out for a walk, dimly conscious something fucked-up was afoot.

I took the bus back, trekking a few blocks to Westlake Mall. Political fliers were still scattered everywhere. That week between leaf blowing season and the moment all the Christmas lights go up, somebody had thoughtfully turned off the fountains, more to keep them from getting clogged with leaves than from freezing—the air was dense with a warm film of fog keeping the bite off your cheeks as you walked. I shoved my gloves in my back pocket walking past Borders, scoping out the windows—nada.

At the break of the millennium, I was thinking, the people of the world's most powerful land were asked to choose a leader, but at the last minute couldn't decide. When it came time to vote, there was a huge sense of ambivalence. Maybe they'd spent October holed up watching reality programs, subscribing to easy-reading newspapers. Maybe the election had been set too close to a major holiday, when they were busy shopping and eating tacos and calzones in mall food courts. They'd decided democracy was a pain in the ass no one needed anymore. Maybe they weren't wrong. Having money and democracy at once is like having an itch you're dying to scratch but can't, for politeness's sake. I'm not going to get political here.

That night, after the last voting rallies emptied from the square in front of Westlake Mall, not long before I left for another place I hoped might mean something else, I decided, making a tour through the square, not ready to go home yet, to stop for a drink.

The Eagle isn't like other bars. I saw right away it

hadn't changed in the time I'd been gone. They don't play music to make the clientele dance, and the people playing pool actually play pool, instead of standing around chalking their sticks and looking at each other. They serve beer in a Mason jar. Then, since there's never any space at the bar, you lean against a wall. It's a good bar, and the way it hadn't changed, still a little dirty, was reassuring, almost wholesome. Leaned against a wall slurping beer over the lip of my Mason jar, I saw a guy coming down the stairs. A big, pale guy, dark-rimmed glasses. You could tell by his bare arms, the heavy set of his shoulders, the way he held his Coke bottle in two fingers, he was either smart and precise, compensating with four nights a week at the gym, or else had been the kid who tried to force puzzle pieces into spaces they didn't belong, and was playing smart with the glasses, which were, either way, flattering.

Ten minutes later, watching him go up the stairs, monster calves below the plaid flannel shirt tied at waist, I followed. I'd never followed a man around a bar before, but there was something, maybe the flannel shirt and the bad glasses or just the way he stood that was like everything I'd thought Seattle was when I first got there. Maybe that's what people are about, some of us, chasing after a person who meant something once. Places the same way, too. Maybe everything is. After a while we were talking, standing with our arms touching. We went downstairs to get another drink. The bar's door hung ajar to the rain. A little wet air came in from outside. Then it slammed open, letting in a small crowd, which is when I saw Trent.

He'd seen me first. He said we needed to talk some time, and I said *yeah*, but he was with some people, and I guess he saw I was, too. So we stood there. Then he was gone and I had my hand on the bar with the wet air coming in from the door and when the beer came, leaning back against the wall, all the light of heaven shone in that little bar, like I was right in the middle of something pushing into the walls from every side, a way I hadn't felt in a long time. And it wasn't just the beer, because I'd drunk enough beer between then and now to know what beer can do for you is actually pretty limited.

My guy with the arms and flannel and I stood around on a kind of catwalk over the rest of the bar. He'd introduced me to the people he was with, a guy named Kevin, a faster-talking version of my guy himself, and a couple in costumes who were acting like it was Halloween. After a while it worked like this: I had a decent couple of lines of conversation with Kevin on one side, then turned back to my guy to make out until he said something, which was usually about how he couldn't stand bars, or felt like his body was totally out of shape, then turned back to Kevin for a little meaningful conversation until you could tell my guy was bored fiddling with his Coke bottle, staring into space, and it seemed like time to make out again. Things went like that for a while. In the meantime their friends hung close to us. There was a semi-drunk guy in spray-on latex and devil's horns and angels' wings, which seemed to be of real feathers because every time he backed up against a candle somebody had to put it out, but it was nice because it kind reminded you it had been Halloween.

I looked across the bar for Trent. He didn't seem to be anywhere. "There's a patio outside," said my guy, trying to be helpful. I'd tried explaining about Trent. I'd tried three times, tried like a person might when he's trying to explain something he can't quite grasp after a couple of beers. Every time I'd try, I'd get out as much as "we were on a boat together." Then my guy would want to know what boat and how I knew people with a boat, wishing he knew them too, and there was no way to separate out the easy parts and if there was a story about it I couldn't tell where it started or ended or how to sum it up. But my guy didn't care much as long as I kept one hand on his forearm, the other making occasional forays up the small of his back. He said *yeah* he'd seen Trent before. He was a pretty well-known as a character in the bars.

I went out to the patio and back. After a while, Trent and his friends came upstairs, taking our spot. Crowding from the sides pushed us closer. He turned, raising an eyebrow. I looked him in the eyes. His face hardened to a firm grin, pushing close, shifting his eyes as they focused on mine, mirroring whatever he picked up in my own face. His grin widened, pressing closer, his expression a sudden copy of my own so exact that I felt its outline in the muscles of my own jaw. He held this look, pushing his face to mine, leaving me a second to register it, then another to be sure, pulling his face away, looking back as he went out the door below.

Downstairs, Kevin and the guy with wings were trying to tell me what a nice guy my guy was. "Normally it's Kevin who meets guys, and I just stand around," my guy said.

We passed the all-night tattoo parlor, darkened antique shop windows, the highway overpass, the Sharper Image and Borders, the FAO Schwartz and finally the market and my own street with its crying gulls and rush of wet car tires on asphalt. He left. I retraced my steps, following the monorail along Fifth Avenue, finding myself in that long wasteland of broken warehouses out by the lake, walking to the lake, turning right, swinging past a Burger King along the edge of the lake, finding myself at the dock that led to Trent's houseboat.

To say there was nothing there would be true enough. There wasn't a gaping space, a flat plane of dark water where the houseboat had floated. It still floated there in the most basic sense. A couple of lit windows, one in the kitchen and one up somewhere in the loft. A television flickered behind the blinds, lighting the pier, series of blurred blue shudders.

I walked to the end of the dock for a look at the lake. Turning uphill, bits of shatter-proof glass sparkled under a streetlight on the asphalt. The roofline of my old building hung above freeway overpass columns and a sweep of low brush. The homeless guy stretched out on our bench, dreaming of angels and devils and temples submerged under Elliot Bay, the state of his soul, checked at some imaginary party long ago, misplaced in the cloakroom. If he'd come in with one to begin with. None of this was quite like I've written it, but it's all as true as can be.

It was late. One last thing on the hill still seemed open—this one little cafe. From below, you could make out an empty booth inside, lit up behind the plate glass. I'd never noticed it before that night. I'm still not sure how I could have missed it.

Acknowledgments

The author wishes to thank Erin Goedhart-Stallings and Louis Flint Ceci for their comments on this book's manuscript, and the publishers of *Callisto* and *Interdisciplinary Studies in Literature and Environment*, in which excerpts from this novel first appeared in slightly different form.

About the Author

J. M. Parker's fiction has appeared in the journals *Callisto, Chelsea Station, Foglifter, Gertrude, ISLE, SAND* and *Segue*, among others, and has been reprinted in *Best Gay Stories 2015*. He is the author of *A Budget Traveler's Guide to the Museums of Europe*, a novel; and *Blossoms in Snow: Austrian Refugee Poets in Manhattan*, a volume of translated poetry. He lives in Salzburg, Austria, where he teaches creative writing and American studies.